SORCERESS

Maggie Furey lives in County Wicklow in the Republic of Ireland with her husband Eric and their cats. She is the author of the *Artefacts of Power* series, which in less than five years has made her one of the bestselling fantasy authors in the UK.

SERIES EDITOR
Simon Spanton

For more information about the books,
competitions and activities, check out our website:
http://www.orionbooks.co.uk/web

THE WEB
SORCERESS

◆

MAGGIE FUREY

Dolphin Paperbacks

To the cats, forever loved:
To Owen and Amy, last of the six, and to the memory
of Boswell, Lucy, Spice and Rose.

First published in Great Britain in 1998
as a Dolphin paperback
by Orion Children's Books
a division of the Orion Publishing Group Ltd
Orion House
5 Upper St Martin's Lane
London WC2H 9EA

Typeset at The Spartan Press Ltd,
Lymington, Hants
Printed and bound in Great Britain by
Clays Ltd, St Ives plc.

A catalogue record for this book is available
from the British Library
Printed in Great Britain
ISBN 1 85881 551 7 (pb)

CONTENTS

CHAPTER ONE

KNIGHTFALL

The knight rode into the clearing on his white horse. The sun, very bright in a blue sky, glinted on his armour, forcing him to squint his eyes against the glare. The suit of polished steel felt heavy and hot but the knight was glad of it. He hoped it would be enough to protect him from the deadly monster lurking in the dark, thick forest that surrounded him on all sides.

The clearing seemed as good a place as any to stop. There was no real need to hunt the creature – sooner or later, it would find him. The white charger fidgeted for a while and then, because it sensed no danger, it put its head down and started to eat the grass. The knight let the reins go slack but stayed alert, never taking his eyes from the gloomy shadows beneath the trees. The horse could rest, but he could not. He was tense with a mixture of excitement and fear. This was the biggest challenge of his life. He had never fought a dragon before.

Suddenly, the horse lifted its head. A loud crashing and the sharp crack of breaking branches came from the depths of the woods. The knight could see the treetops toss and sway as if a high wind was blowing through them – and then all other sounds were drowned out by a loud, furious bellow. Before the knight could take another breath, an awesome, terrifying creature burst out of the forest.

The dragon's head, on a long, slender neck, almost reached the tops of the trees. Its massive jaws were filled with teeth like long, curving steel knives. Its skin was made up of glimmering scales of green and gold, and when it opened its great wings, ribbed and leathery like those of a gigantic bat, they blocked out the sun. Its eyes, like two huge glittering rubies, looked down at the knight with a cold, insect-like gaze. The knight took a deep breath, braced his lance into position, and charged.

The dragon screamed with rage, and leaped to one side, away from the sharp wooden lance. As it turned, one great wing caught the knight a glancing blow, making his horse stumble and almost sweeping him from the saddle. He rocked and lurched, almost falling, but managed to pull himself back into place before the horse reached the far side of the clearing. Taking a tighter grip on the lance, he gathered the reins in his left hand, swung the horse around, and charged again.

The monster lowered its head, its glittering gaze sweeping across the knight. To his dismay, two thin red beams came sizzling from the dragon's eyes and met just in front of him, burning the tip of his lance to ash. The knight gasped in horror. So much for the legend that dragons could breathe fire. *This* dragon was using lasers!

Angrily, the knight threw away the smouldering stub of his lance and made a desperate grab for his sword. It slid free from his scabbard with a clang. The dragon waited for him at the other side of the clearing, crouched in a fighting pose with its great wings fanning the air and its ruby eyes glowing. Spurring his horse, the knight galloped towards it. Without the longer reach that the lance gave him, he would have to get very close to the dragon to use his sword – well within reach of those fearsome jaws. This would be his last chance.

The dragon bellowed its rage and rose up on its hind feet with a fearsome hiss, towering higher and higher into the blue sky. The knight's heart leaped. If he could get in one good blow and stab the sword into its soft underside, he could kill the brute. But the dragon was too quick. Before he could get close enough, its long spiny tail curved round and lashed out at him, knocking him from the saddle with a deafening clatter of armour. The sword was knocked from his hand and lost in the long grass. His horse gave a terrified neigh and galloped away to vanish amongst the trees. The knight lay stranded on his back, helpless in his clumsy armour. He watched the dragon's massive jaws, with their wickedly sharp teeth coming down towards him, opening wider and wider . . . Though he knew better, he could not help closing his eyes to shut out the ghastly sight – and when he opened them again, the dragon had changed into a laughing, dark-haired girl with flashing brown eyes. .

'Wipeout!' she shouted.

For a moment, Jack was angry with her for making a fool of him, but then his sense of fairness won out. There was no denying it, she had beaten him fair and square, and he had never seen a better dragon. He grinned back at her and stood up, tapping a code into the keypad on his wrist to make his armour vanish. 'Whoo! Hair-y, Leni. What a monster. It was so *real*! You been working on your animals in secret?'

'Sort of,' Eleni said shyly. 'Anna helped me a bit with the dragon shape, and I've been taking some advice from the Cat—'

'That would explain why your dragon moves so well. You keep that up, and one day the Cat is going to get a big surprise.'

'Oh, I don't know about that,' Eleni said shyly. She'd been the proud owner of a full Websuit for a short while only. Before that, she had known nothing but the limited world of glove and glasses. It was taking some time for her shyness to wear off, but in the Web you could be anything you wanted. With the help of her friends, Jack included, she was growing braver every day. Why, before long, she would be as confident as Rom . . . Jack caught himself up with a chuckle. That would be the day, when anyone could outbite that wise-ass Rom.

Eleni was talking again. 'I thought I would use the dragon as my usual shape in the Web for a while. What do you think?'

'I think it's a brilliant idea! There's all sorts of things we could do.'

'What sort of things?' asked a cool little voice. Eleni and Jack turned to see a grey tabby cat sitting in the grass, watching them with round green eyes. A small blue-green hummingbird buzzed around its head.

'Cat!' Jack greeted her with delight. 'My sprite – did it find you?' He was very proud of the sprite. The little hummingbird was still very much a test model, but it seemed to be working very well.

The Cat flicked her ears at the hovering bird. 'It was waiting for me on Level 1,' she said. 'It found me at once. It's the most useful new invention I've seen in a long while. I'm sure they'll catch on.'

Jack could hear the envy in her voice, and tried not to feel smug. 'You're right.' He keyed a code into his wristpad, and the hummingbird vanished in a flash of blue. 'Sprites make it easy to find people in the Web. I'm sure it won't be long before we all have one.'

The Cat sighed. 'You don't know how lucky you are, Jack, living next door to someone who designs amazing stuff like this.' With a flip of her tail, as if to change the subject, she turned to the Greek girl. 'Hi, Leni.'

'*Yiasou*, Cat,' said Eleni. 'What do you think of the dragon?' Keying her wristpad, she took on the dragon's shape again. She turned to the side and unfolded her great wings.

'Your tail could do with being a bit longer,' the Cat replied.

'Is that all you've got to say?' Jack demanded. 'Don't you think it's great?'

The Cat twitched her tail. 'It's more than great, it's eight! But Leni asked me to help her get it right, and that's what I'm doing.' She turned to the Greek girl. 'Did you beat him, then?'

'Knocked him right out of his saddle,' Eleni replied smugly. 'He didn't stand a chance. It's a good thing they don't allow real animals in the Web. If the horse had been alive, instead of just a phace, it would still be running—' She was interrupted by a high-pitched beeping sound. A little green spider, about the size of a football, came scurrying out of the trees and headed for Eleni. The Greek girl flicked back to her human shape and scowled at it. 'It's Mama,' she sighed.

'Six!' muttered Jack. 'Do you have to go yet, Leni? A green spider isn't an urgent call. It's not as if the house was burning down, or anything.'

'She'll want me to help with dinner,' Eleni told him. 'I told you how it is, Jack. In my family, everyone has their own jobs to do. We all have to help. I can come back later, if you like.'

'OK.' Jack pushed impatiently at the spider, who seemed to be trying to climb Eleni's leg. 'I'll try to get some of the others together to see your new shape. I won't tell them who it is – we'll see if they can guess. I'll be here – or if I'm not, I'll send my sprite for you. I'll probably be in the Menagerie.' He grinned at her. 'I'm trying to find a phoenix. I thought it would look good sitting in the fireplace of our castle.'

Ever since the Dreamcastle game had closed, the three of them – Jack, Eleni and the Cat, with some occasional help from Rom – had been trying to build a castle of their own in a rented design space in E&R (Educational and Recreation). Some days the results were better than others.

'What?' Eleni cried. 'How do you propose to *keep* it in the fireplace?'

Jack shrugged. 'We'll think of something.'

Eleni chuckled. 'A phoenix for the fireplace – I like it. What about a mermaid for the moat, too? *Tha sas tho*, Jack,

Cat – see you later.' She hit her scuttle button and exploded, with a soundless 'pop', into a cloud of coloured firework sparks that lingered in the air for a moment, whirling like a snowstorm before they vanished.

'What a shame,' Jack said, when Eleni had gone. 'If it's not helping her mum, it's looking after that pesky little sister of hers. Don't they want her to have *any* fun?'

'Huh!' the Cat said sharply. 'She's not the only one who has to help at home. Eleni gets to spend a lot more time in the Web than *I* do! We aren't all as lucky as you, you know!'

'I suppose not,' Jack agreed. 'I forget sometimes, just how lucky I am.' He shrugged. 'Well, what are we going to do now?'

The Cat stood up and stretched, arching her grey, furry back. 'What about going over to Menagerie and having a look at those fabulous beasties you wanted?'

The Menagerie was a database that contained a virtual replica of every living creature imaginable – some real, some extinct, and others out of pure legend. It could be visited like a zoo, and the animals could be copied, turned into phaces, and used in other areas of the Web.

'Why not?' Jack entered the Menagerie code into his wristpad, watching as the Cat did likewise with a delicate claw. From a distance, her pad looked like part of the tabby markings that spotted her leg, and as always, Jack found himself wondering what she *really* looked like. Of course, it was impossible to tell what anyone looked like while they were in the Web, but most people had at least one human form that was usually a better-looking version of them-selves. The Cat, however, never changed from the shape she was wearing now, and never talked about her life outside the Web. She was a complete mystery.

'What's going on?' The Cat's voice jerked Jack out of his thoughts. He suddenly realized that he was still standing in the forest clearing. He frowned. 'Where's the Menagerie?' he muttered.

'Let's get in from Level 1,' the Cat suggested – but when they spun out to the Education block and into Webtown, it was just the same. They soon found the right skyscraper, but instead of the Menagerie window, there was nothing but a blank grey void.

Jack looked at the Cat. 'That's impossible,' he said. 'A part of the Web can't just disappear! What on earth is happening?'

CHAPTER TWO

THE SILVER WOMAN

There seemed no way at all to get into the Menagerie. It seemed like admitting defeat, to tamely report the fault to the nearest spider, but in the end, that was all they could do. Cat was intrigued and, Jack suspected, a little annoyed by the mystery. She decided to zip over to Tropicana Bay, and see if Rom was hanging out there. If anyone would get to the bottom of it, she suggested, he could. Jack, who had been in the Web for long enough already, knew he should scuttle home and get something to eat before the voms set in. That way he could return to the Web when Eleni came back.

As Jack pressed his scuttle button the surroundings of Webtown wavered and dissolved into a swirling sea of coloured particles. He broke through the surface like a swimmer – and was back in Realworld, the Websuit clinging tightly to his body. Jack blinked at the unfamiliar surroundings. It was always a surprise coming back here, to Anna's spare room. She was his family's nearest neighbour and his mother's best friend, who lived a mile or two down the lane from Jack's own house. He was staying with her while his parents were away, and not minding a bit. Anna Lucas was an exciting and special person – the noted designer of some of the most popular Web games run by the big companies – and because Jack knew her so well, he and his friends were lucky enough to be able to test those games before they went public.

Suddenly realizing just how hungry he was, Jack peeled

off the Websuit, leaving it inside out to air. He dressed in some loose, comfortable old sweats, and went to find some food. He paused in the kitchen to look out of the window at the soft rain sweeping across the hills. Irish weather, he thought. This place never seems to go short of rain – as if the world isn't grey enough when I spin out of the Web. It always took a while to get used to being back in the outside world. Movement after coming out of the Web was like walking through thick syrup. Jack's body felt slow to him, and clumsy. Colours seemed dull and flat, and sounds were slightly muffled. The slows only lasted for about ten minutes or so, while his brain adjusted to the slower 'real-time', but while it was happening it felt weird.

When he reached the kitchen Jack was set upon by three cats who also seemed to think it was a mealtime. Meowling pitifully, they rubbed around his legs as he went towards the fridge. It was like trying to wade through furry water. 'All right, all right,' he told them, and tipped a handful of dried food into their bowls. As usual, they all reacted differently. Max, a huge ball of honey-coloured fur, dived head-first into the bowl as though he had not seen food for days. Maya, also golden but short-haired and spotted with black like a leopard, ate slowly, purring throughout the meal and looking up at Jack from time to time with her huge amber eyes. Khan the Burmese, a sleek dark shadow, turned his nose up at the cat food and leaped up on the table to see what Jack was putting in his sandwich.

'If you were *my* cat—' Jack threatened, scooping Khan back to the floor. The cat gave him a black look, then ignored him completely.

Just as he had finished making the sandwich, Anna came in, blinking and stretching after hours spent in her own Websuit. She looked tired.

'Had a hard day?' Jack asked her.

'You can say that again.' Anna ruffled her fingers through her short, red-gold hair until it stood up in spikes. She keyed the autochef and when the machine pinged, took out a bulb of steaming coffee. The pleasant, bitter smell flooded the kitchen as she broke the seal. 'I'm up to my ears in dragons,' she went on. 'The wretched things won't behave themselves.' She perched on a tall kitchen stool and absent-mindedly took one of Jack's sandwiches. 'It's not so much the dragons themselves,' she went on with a sigh. 'It's the shifters – the creatures I designed to be the enemies of the dragons in the game. Once I taught the little horrors to change shape and go through walls, they started popping in and out all over the place. It's impossible to keep track of them.'

Jack smiled to himself. It wasn't unusual for Anna to talk this way. He was looking forward to her latest creation – Dragonville, she called it. After the highly popular Dreamcastle had been forced to close, the game companies were all looking for a replacement. The designer who came up with something suitable would be able to name their own price. Jack agreed with Anna that Dragonville would be perfect – except that lately, the program seemed to have developed a mind of its own, and was going off in all sorts of directions its designer had *not* intended.

Speaking of which . . . 'Hey! Did you know the Menagerie application has gone right down the plug? It's impossible to get into it. All we're getting is a kind of weird grey wall.'

Anna looked up from her coffee. 'That's strange. It's not the only glitch I've heard of lately, either. I wonder what's going on? The Web seems full of gremlins, including my uncontrollable shifters.' She glowered at the drinking bulb as though it was somehow to blame, then brightened up. 'How did Eleni's dragon work, by the way? Wasn't she planning to try it out on you today?'

Jack made a face. 'It worked just fine. She smeared me all over the place. I bet those laser eyes were your idea.'

Anna laughed. 'Just something I'm working on for Dragonville. You might say Eleni was testing them for me.

She promised to keep them secret, apart from you and the Cat. Oh, I nearly forgot. I have a present for her, to celebrate her new Websuit.' She put down the uneaten sandwich, fished in her pocket and held out a scrap of paper with a series of numbers on it, and what looked like a tiny, glittering blue button. 'There you are, slot this into the input port in your wrist unit and get Eleni to enter this code in her own keypad, followed by her personal access code. It's her very own sprite—' she grinned. 'A real one this time. Just wait till you see it.'

'Wow, eight!' Jack's hug nearly knocked her off the stool. 'Thanks, Anna. Eleni will be so pleased – and another sprite will come in really useful.' He grinned. 'All those vets and phreaks will be venom-green with envy!'

Anna laughed. 'Well, you show them off as much as you like. It'll be good advertising for me, and the more these little critters get tested out, the better it is.'

'There'll be some fun and games when everybody has one.' Until now, Jack owned the only sprite in the Web. Sprites were phaces that took the shapes of small flying creatures. If Jack wanted to meet one of his friends, say Eleni, he could key her personal access code into his wristpad. If she was in the Web, the sprite would find her and lead her back to him. In time, Anna hoped to program them to carry messages.

'Is it the same as mine? A hummingbird?' he asked.

Anna shook her head. 'No. I'm not telling you what it is. Let it be a surprise. I have one for your friend the Cat, too.' She handed him another button, red this time. 'Her sprite is different again.'

'She'll love that.' Jack knew that Anna had a soft spot for the Cat. He supposed it was because she had such a thing about the Realworld animals.

'I would do one for Rom, but by the time I get around to it, he'll probably have worked out how to make one for himself.' She raised her eyebrows severely. 'Mind, you make sure and tell him I don't want to see any pirate sprites flying around the Web.'

'You know he wouldn't do that.'

'I know. He's far too fond of testing out the new games to mess about with my designs.' She grinned. 'I'm going to Tropicana Bay later, to meet your mum. Any messages?'

'Just the usual love and stuff,' Jack told her. 'If I hadn't promised to meet Eleni, I would have come with you. Isn't Dad tired of touring yet?' Jack's father was a musician who played old classical rock – dinosaur music, Jack called it. Most of his performances were done from home, through the Web, but from time to time he would go off on tour to play live concerts for those rare few who could afford the price of a ticket – mostly millionaires and heads of state.

'They've had about enough of it by now,' Anna said. 'Your dad says travelling about is much easier inside the Web. Still, they have another three weeks to go, so we'll just have to be patient.' She yawned. 'I'm off for a shower and a nap now. Those wretched shifters have almost finished me off.'

'I'll see you later, then,' Jack said. 'I'm meeting Eleni and the Cat at our castle. I can't wait for them to see their new sprites.'

'I hope *they* work out as they're supposed to.' Anna's face brightened. 'Listen, how would you and the gang like to come with me tomorrow and have a sneak preview of Dragonville? I should be up to the testing phase soon, once I've sorted out the problems with the shifters. I'd like to know what you think of it – see if you can spot anything I've forgotten.'

'Do you mean it?' Jack said. He hadn't expected to see the new game so soon. 'Thanks, I'd love to, and so will the others.' He grinned. 'Rom will be like a dog with two tails. He didn't expect to get a look at your dragons for ages yet.'

'Not to mention the shifters,' Anna said. 'I'd like to see what he makes of them. At the moment they're even more tricky than he is.'

'I'll go and tell them now. I'm supposed to be meeting Eleni in a while in any case. 'See you later, Anna.'

'Don't stay up too late,' she said automatically. See you.' She took a bite of the sandwich in her hand, and her face changed. 'Jack! Peanut butter and *tuna*?'

Eleni finished her chores, then walked down to the end of the garden and looked out across the still waters of the harbour. In the curve of the bay behind her, the sun was setting behind the old monastery, high on its hill. The evening was utterly still, except for the lapping of water against the rocks and the cheeping of the little frogs up in the olive grove.

'When I was your age, the whole of Paleo used to come alive at this time of night.'

Eleni jumped at the voice, and turned to see uncle Kostas coming down the path. He stopped beside her and looked out over the ocean.

'When this place was a tourist resort,' he said, 'you could walk around the bay and hear the music from a dozen different tavernas. The air was filled with the smell of good food, and people would walk up and down the road all evening, talking and laughing.' He sighed. 'Oh, it was fine – before the Web came and killed it all. No one but the rich takes holidays now, and they go to more exotic places than this.'

Eleni frowned. 'But you use the Web. And if you hate it, why did you buy me the Websuit?'

Uncle Kostas laid a hand on her shoulder. 'Ah, Eleni-mou. I can't afford to hate the Web. That's where the future is. As you grow up, all the great opportunities will be there. As for the older folk, like your grandparents – well, the easy money, the tourist money, is gone. Some are going back to the old ways – the fishing, and growing olives and grapes. The younger people – the ones with any sense – do what you are doing. They take advantage of the Web.'

Eleni went back through the quiet garden and into the house. As she climbed into her Websuit, she thought about what uncle Kostas had said. I wonder what *my* future will be, she thought. Maybe I could design games, like Anna, when I grow up. Jack thinks my dragon is pretty good. She decided to go and practise it again. She pulled down her visor, keyed her wristpad, and spun into the Web.

When the flat golden plain of Level 1 stretched out before her, Eleni began to make her alterations. She found 'dragons' on Panel A of her wristpad, and keyed the shape she had invented earlier. Her body grew in size, and her arms dropped down to become legs with huge clawed feet. Wings sprouted from her back, and a long, spiked tail appeared behind her. She liked the feeling of it lashing back and forth.

Wearing the shape of the dragon, Eleni went towards the red E&R block. She was almost there when the blue Exploration block next to it began to ripple, and a woman stepped out. She was dressed from head to foot in a tight suit of shining silver, and a featureless silver mask hid her entire face. Her dark hair streamed out behind her like a cloud, and on her finger glittered a gold ring with a large red stone. She looked as though she was in a hurry but when she saw Eleni she stopped.

'What are *you* doing here?' she asked sharply.

Eleni was about to tell the woman that she must be mistaken, when she realized that she was still wearing the body of a dragon. This woman had mistaken her for some other *dragon*. How peculiar!

'I told you,' the woman snapped impatiently. 'You shouldn't be out here, someone will see you. Get back to the labyrinth at once, you stupid creature.' Then she saw Eleni's wristpad. 'Where did you get that?' she demanded. Leaping forward, she made a grab for the girl's wrist, but Eleni leaped back out of the way and made a dive towards the E&R block. The red surface rippled and parted, and when the blue light cleared, Eleni was standing in Webtown. She wasn't safe yet, however. There was a loud pinging chime, and when she turned, she could see the air above the blue-circled Entry Point beginning to waver. The woman was coming through behind her!

CHAPTER THREE

THE WARNING

Eleni wanted to run, but the avenue was too full of people. Then she remembered. Dragons can fly! She flapped her great wings frantically and sprang up into the air, skimming dangerously low over the heads of the crowd. She soared up between the buildings, wobbling unsteadily from side to side until she got the hang of level flight. After the first terrifying minute she really began to enjoy it. It was like swimming, only a hundred times better. She could enjoy a whole new view of the Webtown, sprawling into the apparent distance like a city with its blocks and interlinking strands.

Below, moved crowds of people, mostly in human shape, but all of them young and beautiful. Many had tinted their skins with brightly coloured designs, and their hair varied through all colours of the rainbow. Some preferred the form of weird-looking alien creatures, while others wore all manner of animal guises, though Eleni could see nothing quite as dramatic as her dragon.

Thinking of her dragon-shape, Eleni reminded herself sharply that this was no time to be playing. Once she was well out of sight of the entry point, she looked for an open space and came down again between two blocks. Fumbling at her wristpad with clumsy claws, she was about to hit the scuttle button when she changed her mind. Who was that woman, anyway? What did she want with a dragon? Instead of spinning out, Eleni tapped in the code to change to her normal human form. Looking like an ordinary girl once more, she hurried back down the crowded strands towards the Entry Point.

The silver woman was still there, just beyond the blue entry area, walking back and forth through the crowds and looking carefully at all the faces. At the sight of the woman's featureless mask, a shiver went through Eleni. The mysterious figure looked all the more sinister because her expression was hidden. Eleni was certain that she could feel herself being fixed by invisible eyes. Suddenly, she was afraid that the woman would recognize her, even though she had changed her shape. Ducking back out of sight around a corner, she keyed in the code for the design space she shared with Jack and the others, and left Webtown in a flash of blue.

Once she had reached the safety of the rented site, Eleni decided to put the strange woman out of her mind. Forget about it, she told herself. If you stop using the dragon you'll be perfectly safe. It was a pity, but surely she could think of something else. To distract herself, she took a good look at the castle she and her friends had been building. It's still not quite right, she thought. Is it because there's no background yet? The castle rested, square and solid, on a flat golden plain that looked much the same as Level 1. Later, when they had finished the building itself, they would put in grass and trees – or perhaps the castle could be in the mountains, or on a cliff overlooking the sea. The choices in the Shaper's data banks were endless.

Everyone who owned a Websuit could rent design space, though a lot of people didn't use them much, preferring their entertainment ready-made. The site acted as a private area that could be designed and changed to suit the user's needs. Any kind of scenery could be chosen from the various extensive databases – desert, jungle, or even another planet. Any kind of building, from a cave to a cottage to a mansion, could be put into place. Animals, too, could be chosen from the Menagerie data banks – anything from ordinary dogs, cats, cows and chickens, to gryphons, basilisks or unicorns.

'Yo, Leni!' Someone was yelling at her from the top of the castle walls.

Eleni looked up and saw a small green frog-like alien waving at her from the battlements. 'Rom!' she shouted. 'Just a minute, I'll come up.'

She crossed the drawbridge over the still-empty moat and went through the tall arched doorway into the castle. The great hall was enormous with carved pillars, a sweeping staircase that would be great for sword fights, and a fireplace big enough to stand in – yet there was something missing. They had copied the building from the 'castle' section of the data banks, but so far it was just a structure. It needed cobwebs and bats, some half-melted candles, secret passages, dungeons and ghosts. She could hardly wait for Jack to come, so that they could get started.

At least the castle had a tower. They had programmed that the last time they had come. Eleni went up the narrow spiral stairs that had been her own idea, and out of the little door at the top that led on to the flat tower roof.

Rom came bouncing towards her. 'Hi, Leni. Where you been hiding? Haven't seen you for a while.'

'Hi.' Eleni had always felt very shy in front of Rom, the ultra-confident Web-wizard, but, today, something had changed. It must have been the dragon, she decided. How could you be shy when you could become something that big and impressive?

Even though Eleni had sworn, not twenty minutes before, never to use the dragon shape again, she found she just couldn't resist it. It would be really eight to be able to show off, for once, to Rom. She grinned at him. 'I've been busy, Rom. Working on a new shape. Like to see it?'

'Sure. I'm always in the market for new shapes.'

Eleni glared at him, pretending to be fierce. 'You keep

your little green paws *off* my new shape! You have quite enough of your own.'

'Peace, peace!' Rom held his little green paws up in front of him. 'You can't hit a guy when he's short and green! Go on, Leni, show me.'

'All right,' Eleni laughed. 'Stand back, Rom, and I mean *well* back.' She entered the dragon code into the keypad on her wrist. The usual, ordinary girl shape that she was wearing shimmered and broke up into a thousand glittering particles that exploded outward and then came swirling back again in the form of a new, much bigger creature. Eleni stretched her huge, green-gold wings and laughed. 'Well? What do you think?'

'Wow!' Rom had stepped back even further, his wide mouth hanging open. A long, scarlet ribbon of tongue unrolled from his mouth, and he jumped as though someone had pinched him and stuffed it back with both hands. The little green alien vanished in a swirl of glitter and Rom's human shape appeared. He was staring so hard that Eleni felt embarrassed. She let the dragon dissolve and spin away, and went back to her human form. 'Do you really like it?' she asked.

'It's eight! I've put on all kinds of shapes, but never anything that *big*. Would you mind if I tried a dragon too? I bet between us, we could come up with some beauties – scare the MIP's out of Jack and the Cat, eh?'

Eleni could have burst with delight. It took some doing to impress Rom, but it seemed she had finally succeeded. At last, she felt as though she truly belonged in the world of the Web.

The urge to show off just a little more was irresistible. 'I don't know about Jack and the Cat, but I certainly fooled some woman in Level 1 today,' she said. 'She mistook me for somebody else entirely.' Eleni frowned as she remembered the woman trying to snatch at her wrist. 'She wore this weird silver suit and a shiny mask with no face. It was horrible.'

She shuddered. 'She had me scared for a minute,' she confessed. 'I don't see how it would be possible for somebody to take my keypad in the Web, but— Rom, what would happen to someone who got stuck in the Web without their wrist unit?'

Rom looked at her, his face very serious. 'It's horrible,' he said quietly. 'It happened to some kids a while ago . . .'

Eleni listened while he told her of his friend Ana Devi, and the ghostly forms of the poor beggar-children of India who had been trapped in the Web for months at a time without any way to escape. 'Eventually, you die,' he told her sadly, 'but it seems to be a long, slow, terrible way to go.'

'What happened to the old woman who kidnapped those children?' Eleni asked.

Rom shrugged. 'In the end we stopped her. Her house burned down and her equipment was destroyed. But she survived, and she's been seen in the Web from time to time. I think she's still trying to find a way to stay here, even when her body dies. If you ever see her, Leni, get away as fast as you can. She's dangerous. I mean it.'

'How would I know her?' Eleni asked curiously. 'This is the Web, Rom. She could look like anything. She could even look like *you*, if she wanted.'

'Oh, you'd know her all right,' Rom replied. 'For some reason, she always gives herself away. No matter what she looks like, she always wears a ring with a huge red stone. You can't possibly miss— Whatever's the matter, Leni?'

'I've seen it,' Eleni whispered. 'It was her, Rom – the woman who tried to steal my keypad. The silver woman! It was *her*!'

CHAPTER FOUR

THE GREEN-EYED CAT

Even as Rom and Eleni looked at each other in horror, the view in front of them wavered. Jack stepped into the scene, as though he had pushed his way through an invisible curtain. 'Hey, Rom, it's been a while. Hey, Leni, you got here,' he called. 'Good. Are you coming down, or shall I come up?'

'We'll come down,' Rom called back. 'We have something to tell you.'

'Eight. And I have something to tell *you*.' From Jack's grin, he clearly hadn't noticed the grim expressions on their faces. 'Did you see the Cat?' he added. 'She was looking for you.'

'No,' yelled Rom. 'Must have missed her. Come on,' he said to Eleni. He grabbed her hand, and they left the roof together.

When they came out of the great castle door, Jack was standing near the drawbridge. 'I have—' he started, but Rom interrupted him.

'Hold on, Jack. Listen. Something's happened. Something serious.'

Jack knew most of the old woman's history in the Web – Rom had told him before. When he heard that she had threatened Eleni, he frowned. 'We had better be careful,' he said. 'Leni, you say it was the dragon she seemed to recognize?'

Eleni nodded. 'She asked me how I had managed to get

out, and what I was doing on Level 1. Then she told me to get back to the labyrinth.'

'Labyrinth? What labyrinth?' Jack muttered.

'One thing is clear,' Rom said. 'She has a dragon – or rather, someone or something in the shape of a dragon – imprisoned there. I wonder what she's up to?'

'I hope we never have to find out,' Eleni said firmly. 'Not if she's *that* dangerous. I don't mind admitting that she scared me. We always trust the Web to be safe.'

Jack was frowning. 'There's something else.' He told them about the disappearance of the Menagerie.

'Do you think there could be a connection?' Eleni asked.

Rom nodded. 'It must be more than a coincidence that the two things should happen on the same day. I can't think what the old woman would want with the Menagerie. Seriously, though, we ought to keep an eye on the situation.'

'Well, forget her for now,' Jack told her. 'Just be careful about turning into a dragon, Leni, unless someone else is with you. Rom, why don't you mention this to what's-her-name, that Webcop you know?'

'Ariadne,' Rom said. 'Yes, I might just do that. I don't think we need mention it to our spiders though. Agreed?'

All three of them looked at one another. They all knew how parents could be. For some reason, adults got far too worried about things, and no one wanted to see any limits on their time in the Web.

'Agreed,' the others chorused.

Rom grinned. 'In the meantime, don't let it spoil our day. What were you saying when you spun in, Jack? You wanted to tell us something.'

Jack's grin came back. 'Anna says do we want to go with her tomorrow and take a look at the new game?'

Eleni let out a whoop of joy.

'Do we *want* to? Do we ever!' shouted Rom.

'Tomorrow morning, then,' Jack said. 'We'll meet you at Tropicana Bay. I have something else here,' he went on, pleased to be able to surprise them further. 'It's a present for Leni. A surprise. Leni, hold out your hand.'

Eleni came forward curiously.

'Now,' Jack said. 'Key this code into your wristpad, and follow it up with your PAC.'

For a minute, Eleni's hand seemed to blur, then she gasped with delight. There, on her palm, stood a tiny, perfect fairy.

Rom let out his breath in a long whistle. 'Wow, Jack. Hairy! Did Anna program that?'

Jack nodded. 'It's a sprite like my hummingbird. If you ever need Rom or me – or anyone else for that matter – you'll be able to send this for us, Leni. Wherever we are in the Web it'll find us. Anna said she'd make one for you, Rom, if you wanted – but you'd probably figure it out for yourself first.'

Rom grinned. 'You never know. I love her inventions, though. She's a real wizard.'

He held out a hand towards the fairy, but it wouldn't come to him. The slender little creature was about as tall as Eleni's longest finger, and glowed with a pinkish gold light that seemed to come from within its own body. It had a set of shimmering double wings like a dragonfly, coloured misty purple and shades of blue, and so delicate that the light shone through them.

'Oh, Jack!' Eleni was lost for words. As she opened her hand a little further, the fairy sprang upwards and took to the air, its wings a silvery blur as it hovered in front of her.

Suddenly, a sleek grey shape exploded out of nowhere. Flailing white paws clawed the fairy out of the air.

'Cat!'

'No!'

'Stop it!'

All three of them shouted at once. The fairy escaped the flashing white paws of the grey tabby cat and flew up again, its blurring wings making an angry buzz.

The Cat glared at it and waved her tail sulkily. 'Well, the

stupid thing was asking for it, hovering there like that. Anyway, what are you making such a fuss about? I didn't hurt it.'

'It was a real basement-level thing to do,' Jack told her angrily.

'Why do you want to spoil things, Cat?' Eleni asked.

'Oh, shut up about your stupid sprite,' the Cat snarled. She turned her back on them and started licking a paw.

'There's no need to be jealous,' Jack told her. 'Anna made one for you, too.'

The Cat's head swivelled sharply. 'She made a sprite for me?' Her green eyes lit up with eagerness.

'Of course. Did you think she'd leave you out? Here, I just need your PAC.'

The expression on the Cat's furry face did not – could not – change, but her tail lashed back and forth faster than ever. 'Oh, curl up, Jack,' she snapped. 'I don't want one of your stupid sprites.' Then she hit her scuttle button and was gone.

Jack, Rom and Eleni looked at each other in dismay, then Jack scowled furiously. 'Why, the stuck-up little—'

'No, Jack.' Eleni shook her head. 'Something upset her. I wonder what's wrong?'

'Who knows? Who cares?' Jack was still frowning. 'Talk about ungrateful. I'll get Anna to reprogram that sprite for Rom.'

'No, wait a while,' Rom urged him. 'You know how moody the Cat can be. she'll probably be all right when she comes back.'

'If she's going to act like that,' Jack muttered darkly, 'she'll be lucky if we have her back at all.'

The scene swirled and exploded into glittering fragments. When Cat lifted up her visor, she was back in her dim, dingy cubicle in the Cybercafe. She pressed the button marked RELEASE and her token sprang back out of the slot and into her hand. Well, at least today's session hadn't cost her much. With movements made jerky by anger, she peeled off her Websuit and threw it down on the couch. By the time Cat reached the door, she had to wipe the blur of tears from her eyes. It's not fair, she thought. It only used to be me, Rom and Jack, before Eleni butted in. Oh, *why* did she have to get that new Websuit?

It hadn't been so bad before. When Eleni had only been gag, Cat hadn't felt so bad about her own problem. She'd done odd jobs for the neighbours every day to earn the money for Cybercafe tokens. But now that the Greek girl had her own suit, she and the boys could spend as much time as they liked in the Web, and Cat would be left out. She was at a disadvantage already – without a suit she couldn't have the sprite, because she didn't have a personal access code. And how could she explain? They must never find out she had no suit of her own, because then she would have to tell them about Dad, and she didn't want them to pity her – it was more than she could bear.

Lurking in the doorway, Cat looked carefully up and down the dull, grey street, before slipping out of the Cybercafe, keeping out of the sickly yellow light of the street lamps. If any of the neighbours should discover her guilty secret and let on to Dad, her life wouldn't be worth living. When she had put a little distance between herself and the arcade, she slowed her pace to an innocent stroll, looking in the shop windows as she went. Just as she was heading up the street, there was a shout from behind her. 'Catherine!'

Cat spun round, smothering a guilty gasp. Behind her, striding quickly up the street, was the tall, stick-thin figure of her father.

CHAPTER FIVE

IN THE CATHEDRAL

Maybe it'll be all right, Cat tried to tell herself. Look innocent. Maybe he didn't see you coming out. But there was a furious scowl on his face as he caught up with her, and he grabbed her arm tightly.

'Just what do you think you're doing?' His face was crimson with anger. 'How many times have I told you to stay away from *that* place?' His voice had risen to a shout now, and people nearby were turning to stare. Cat shrank away from him. She had seen him angry before – he seemed to be angry most of the time these days – but she had never seen him as mad as this. She felt fear like a clenched fist in her stomach, but she also felt anger. He had ruined her life for long enough. What right did he have to treat her like this? 'Get *off* me!' she screamed at him and tore her arm out of his grasp. Then she was running, as fast as she could, away up the street, with no idea where she was going.

Cat heard a shout, and the sound of her father's footsteps pounding along the cobbled street behind her. She kept moving, not daring to slow up and look back. He couldn't be far behind. Around her, ordinary shoppers scattered out of the way. She was bumping into people, but there was no time to stop and apologize. With aching legs, Cat ran uphill and through the market square. There were no moving travelways here. Because Durham was an ancient city, the old fashioned shop windows and concrete pavements had been preserved, and vehicles were kept out of the centre. It looked just as it had looked fifty years ago. The street was narrow, with the buildings leaning out at odd angles, and most of the shops sold weird stuff like unpackaged food, handmade clothes, or candles and chunky jewellery. It was like stepping back in time. More history, Cat thought desperately, as she ran along the narrow pavement. I'm so tired of the past. I want to live *now*!

Cat didn't know whether her dad was still behind her, but she didn't dare stop, just in case. She barely noticed where she was going. Sweat dripped, stinging, into her eyes, and she was gasping for breath. The shops and houses that lined the street were just a blur. Suddenly, the buildings on either side of her vanished. Cat tried to look around, and stumbled. Though she caught herself before she fell, she knew she could run no further. Holding her aching side, she glanced back fearfully, but there was no sign of her father.

Looking around, Cat saw that she was standing in a broad, open space. Why, she had run right up the hill to College Green! To her right was the big, blocky shape of the castle. In front of her, across the lawn where the grass was watered with care every day in summer, the massive cathedral loomed against the sky. Floodlit in silvery light, it looked like a fairy palace with its tall pointed windows and great square bell tower. Looking upwards, Cat could see gargoyles, and statues of angels and saints. Sick of history though she was, she never grew tired of the cathedral. It was too old, and too magnificent.

It was also a good place to hide. Cat knew her father would still be looking for her, and it would only be a matter of time before he came up here. Quickly, she ran across the empty green, ignoring the 'keep off the grass' signs with a pang of guilt. A minute later, she was safely inside.

The cathedral was so vast that it didn't feel like being indoors except for the silence, which fell around Cat like a thick, soft blanket. The electric lights were dim, and hung far above, near the arches of the ceiling. A softer, flickering light came from thick white candles in black iron holders that were taller than Cat herself. The walls, with their arches and dizzy balconies, rose up on either side of her like cliffs, and a double row of pillars, carved in zigzags and diamonds, marched away into the distance towards the night-dark eye of the great round window. Cat shivered. Though the place could not be completely empty, for she could hear the echo of distant footsteps, there was no one in sight. She had never been alone here at night before. It was beautiful, but very spooky. Suddenly, she remembered that she was supposed to be hiding. What if Dad should walk in now?

Almost as if the thought had summoned him, Cat heard footsteps coming in at the outer door. Her heart leaped up into her throat. It was impossible to run in the cathedral. For one thing, she'd be thrown out if somone saw her, but also, there was an eerie feeling of *watchfulness* here that made Catherine want to creep around like a mouse. Where could she hide? Then she noticed the dark blue velvet curtain that hid the door to the bell tower. A white board on a post stood in front of it, saying CLOSED FOR REPAIR. It was the ideal place. Forgetting not to run, she darted across and dived behind the thick velvet.

The curtain smelled of dust and age. Its folds would hide her easily, though the tower door would be locked of course. Listening for footsteps, Cat leaned back against the door – and staggered backwards as it swung silently open behind her. Something rolled under her feet, and she sat down hard on the bottom step of the tower's spiral staircase.

It was too good to be true! Someone, a workman probably, had forgotten to lock the door of the bell tower. But what had she fallen over? She groped around in the darkness until her hand came to rest on a scatter of long, smooth objects, so thick that she could barely get her hands around them. Candles! Some wonderful, kindly person had left a supply of candles in the niche at the bottom of the stairs. Now, if only . . . She groped in the niche until she found a shelf, and there, as she had hoped, was an electric lighter. Shielding the flame with her hand, she lit one of the candles, and made her second great discovery. The door of the tower could be bolted from the inside! It was a new bolt, and slid easily and quietly shut. Cat wondered who would have put it there, and why. It wasn't surprising that the tower was being repaired – the old bells hadn't rung for years – but why would anyone want to lock the door from the *inside*?

'Catherine? Catherine!'

Cat held her breath as she heard her father calling. After a moment, she heard another, more quiet voice, 'Sir, do you mind? This is a House of God.'

Her father stamped away, muttering words that were definitely out of place in a cathedral, and Cat heaved a sigh of relief. He would never find her now! She had better stay where she was, though, in case the other person was still hanging about.

It was quite pleasant to sit on the dark tower steps in a cosy circle of candlelight. It was far more peaceful here than at home, Cat decided, thinking about the housing estate and the little house filled to bursting with her three young brothers and a sister. Not to mention Dad, silent, stern and glowering – and filled with bitter hatred for the Web.

When Cat had been very young – too small, really, to remember much about it – her dad had been a teacher of history, but as the Web became more and more advanced, a single person could teach hundreds of kids. Then Websuits were invented, and the old-fashioned lessons vanished for ever. Kids learned by experiencing whatever they were being taught – learning had become an adventure, and a game. It must be tremendous fun, Cat thought wistfully, but the Web had put her dad on the scrap-heap, and he refused to have anything to do with it. He had grown more and more bitter and angry, and after her mum had left he taught Cat and her brothers and sister himself, and didn't seem to know, or care, what they were missing. For the last three years, Cat had been sneaking off to the Cybercafe whenever she had any money, but now he had found her out, she wouldn't even be able to do that.

Cat clenched her fists and forced herself not to cry. I hate him, she thought fiercely. I won't go back. *I'll never go back!*

After a while, though, she began to wonder what else she *could* do. Cat wasn't used to being alone, and she felt guilty that she wasn't at home now, taking care of the younger ones. Would Dad get their tea for them tonight? The thought of tea reminded Cat that she was cold and very hungry. When she heard the voice calling from somewhere up the tower stairs, she thought she must be going mad.

It came softly at first, then louder – the thin, high, quavery voice of an old woman.

'*I see you, child. Why sit down there in the cold, when it's warmer upstairs, in my tower?*'

CHAPTER SIX

THE SORCERESS IN HER TOWER

Who is that? Cat thought in panic. How can she be here? How does she know *I'm* here? It's impossible. And she sounds just like a witch. A shiver went through her. For goodness' sake grow up, she told herself angrily. Fancy believing in witches at your age. 'Who – who's there?' she tried to shout, but the words stuck in her throat, and came out in a whisper.

'A friend, my dear. Come up into the tower and get warm. I'm sure you must be hungry, too.'

At the thought of food, Cat's stomach gave an embarrassing growl. Though she had been told over and over again not to trust strangers, how could a little old lady do her any harm? She sounded kind enough, and, besides, Cat was eaten up by curiosity. Who was this woman? What could she be doing here?

Taking a deep breath and gripping the candle tightly, Cat set off up the steep, worn steps. She climbed and climbed, while the flickering candle made her shadow dance on the cold stone walls. She didn't hear the voice again. The only sounds were the hollow tapping of her feet on the stairs and her breathing, that grew louder and faster as she ascended. Sometimes, she would pass an old wooden door but everyone that she tried was firmly locked. At last, when she thought she must be very near the top, one of the doors came open as she pushed it, and swung inward with a creak.

Cat couldn't believe her eyes. Instead of the bare,

cobwebby stone room that she'd expected, the place was filled with warmth and a dim but cosy red light. There was a carpet on the floor and the windows were covered with thick curtains. Standing at one side of the door, Cat gasped as she looked up at a tall, broad man whose arms and legs were almost as thick as her body.

'It's all right. Don't be afraid of Maxus.'

Cat tore her eyes from the big man to see who had spoken. In the corner, seated in a wheelchair, was an old, old lady. She seemed tiny and frail, and looked lost in the tangle of bottles, tubes and wires attached to her chair, but the proud bones of her face, her thin, jutting hook of a nose, and her sparkling dark eyes gave her a look of arrogance and command. Then, surprisingly, her face broke up into a mass of friendly wrinkles as she smiled.

'Come in, my dear, and get acquainted. I'll get Maxus to heat you some soup.'

Slowly, Cat stepped forward. The old lady's bright, dark eyes held her captive, just like a bird fascinated by a snake. She held out a hand like a bony claw and Cat saw a huge ring with a blood-red stone. The woman smiled again, still holding her hand out in a friendly way, though her eyes glittered fiercely. 'Come to me,' she said softly.

When Cat came close and put her hand in the woman's bony claw, she was amazed at the strength of the grip. The old lady smiled at her. 'You can call me Miss Aldanar, my dear. Now, tell me all about it. Who are you, and why are you hiding here in my tower?'

'*Your* tower?' Cat asked in astonishment. 'But, doesn't it belong to the cathedral?'

'In a sense.' The woman's smile grew broader. 'But shall we just say I'm borrowing it for a while?'

'And they let you?' Cat felt rather shocked.

The woman's smile switched off like a light. '*Let* me? There's no question of whether they'd let me. When, and if, you get to my age, you'll find that enough money can open any door. The upkeep of the cathedral is very expensive, you know. Now—' the smile returned again. 'Sit down here beside me, drink your soup, and tell me what *you* are doing here.'

Cat turned round to see the huge, glowering man standing by her shoulder, holding out a bulb of something that smelled very good indeed. For an instant she hesitated, wondering if the soup was drugged or something. The old woman cackled with laughter. 'If I meant to harm you, do you really think you could get away from Maxus? I wouldn't need to drug you, my dear – or poison you, for that matter.'

Suddenly, Cat felt very silly. The old woman must be lonely, stuck up here with no one but the silent, scowling Maxus for company. The poor old thing was probably a bit batty, but she meant to be kind – and she was a whole lot kinder than Cat's father. 'Thank you very much.' Cat took the bulb from Maxus and sat down on the low stool beside the old lady's wheelchair. 'How did you know I was down at the bottom of the tower?' she asked.

'Security camera.' The woman shrugged, as though it were the most normal thing in the world. 'And I spoke to you through the same system. Now, no more questions. Tell me what you were doing down there.'

Between sips of the hot, delicious soup, Cat began to tell the dismal story of her troubles to her new friend.

'And he won't let you use the Web at *all?*' the woman interrupted.

Cat shook her head. 'He hates everything to do with it.'

'Ridiculous! Why, I don't think it's even legal. You're supposed to have a proper education.'

'Dad teaches us himself.' Cat sighed wistfully. 'From what the other kids tell me, I'm missing out on a tremendous lot.'

'Your father doesn't seem to care that you'll be at a disadvantage when you grow up,' the old lady said sharply. 'The fool! And so you slip away to the Cybercafe whenever you have a chance? Well, good for you.'

Cat couldn't believe it. This woman, this amazing, proud old lady who lived alone in her tower with her faithful servant, just like a sorceress in a fairy tale, understood Cat far better than her own family did. No one had ever been so kind to her – except maybe Jack, she thought, feeling a sudden pang of guilt at the memory of her quarrel with him.

'Well,' the woman was still talking. 'When you ran away, you came to exactly the right place.' Once again, the wrinkled old face creased into a smile. 'As it happens, I might just be able to help you.' She gestured to Maxus, who squeezed behind the wheelchair and pulled at a curtain that was hung right across the corner of the room. It slid aside with a rattle. Cat gasped. I must be dreaming, she thought. There, in the corner, were two foam-form couches – and two truly venomous Websuits.

'I don't need two suits just for myself,' the old lady said kindly. 'I worked in Websuit design right from the very early days, and I still like to keep my hand in. These are a brand new, experimental model. They should have faster reaction times, give you clearer virtual images, *and* be more comfortable to wear. I need someone to help me try them out – so one of these suits is yours for as long as you like, my dear.'

Cat couldn't believe her ears. 'Thank you, oh, thank you,' she whispered. Now she could be like the others! She could stay in the Web as long as she liked, she could see Jack more often. She just kept looking at the Websuits, so happy that she almost wanted to cry. She was far too excited to wonder why the two suits were connected to one another by a mysterious tangle of wires that all went into a small white box with a flashing digital display. She was too busy making plans to notice the expression of avid greed in the old woman's glittering dark eyes – as if *she* were a spider – and Cat was an unsuspecting fly.

CHAPTER SEVEN

DRAGONVILLE

The beach at Tropicana Bay was fairly quiet, though there were quite a few people in the water, surfing the glittering breakers or riding sailboards further out where the ocean was calmer. Others were swimming, or playing with the dolphin phaces that disported themselves among the silvery waves. When Eleni arrived, Jack and Anna were already there, seated at one of the spindly tables that were spread out at the edge of the crimson sands, beneath the yellow-flowered trees.

Anna smiled. 'There you are,' she said. '*Kalimera*, Eleni. *Ti kanis?*'

'Good morning, Anna,' the Greek girl replied with a smile. 'I'm fine, thank you.'

'Now,' Anna said, 'only Rom to come, and the Cat.'

'She isn't coming,' Jack interrupted.

Anna raised an eyebrow. 'Why ever not?'

Jack shrugged. 'I didn't get a chance to tell her,' he confessed. 'We had a fight yesterday. Don't ask me what it was about, 'cos I still don't know. She turned up when I was showing Leni her sprite, and if you want to know the truth, I think the Cat was a bit jealous. But when I told her there was one for her, too, she blew up completely, didn't she, Leni? Spun out in a huff.'

'I've never seen her in such a temper,' Eleni agreed.

'You can say *that* again.' The new voice came from Rom, who had appeared while they were talking.

'Hi, Rom,' Anna said. 'That was good timing. Well, now that everyone's here, let's get going, shall we?'

Eleni followed the others out of Tropicana Bay and back to Level 1. They entered the red Entertainment and Recreation block, and found themselves in the Webtown for that site.

'We'll have to spin in from here,' said Anna, 'I haven't created a proper access yet. Here, I'll give you the codes.'

As she keyed the codes into her wristpad, Eleni felt a flutter of excitement inside. How lucky we are, she thought. A brand new game by such a well-known designer, and we'll be the first to see it! Then she entered the final sequence of the code, and the world around her flickered and *changed*.

Eleni found herself standing on a dizzying ledge, looking out across a vast mountain range with jagged peaks and shadowy canyons that seemed to plunge down deep into the earth. The bare rock of the cliffs and peaks were laid down in layers of red and golden stone, and though Eleni knew that they had only been recently created by Anna, it looked as though they had been weathered into weird, curving shapes by centuries of wind and rain. Many caves had been hollowed into the peaks, their yawning mouths dark against the glowing stone. The sky was more green than blue, and all the shadows had a strange, purple tinge.

Far below, a canyon snaked away between the two nearest mountain peaks, and as Eleni looked down, a speck of silver caught her eye, glowing like a spark among the purple shadows. As it drew nearer, the girl could make out the slender, sinewy shape of the body, the long, slim tail and the great outstretched wings ribbed like those of a gigantic bat. It was a dragon!

Now, other dragons could be seen as sparks of glowing colour – copper, sapphire and glistening emerald green. Flapping their mighty wings to gain extra height, the dragons swept upwards towards Eleni and her friends, growing bigger and bigger, the closer they came.

'They're so beautiful,' Eleni gasped. 'Far more graceful than mine.'

'These have to do more flying,' Anna told her. 'They sort of got more streamlined as time went on.' She tapped something into her wrist unit, the most elaborate keyboard that Eleni had ever seen. Far more complex than those used by the girl and her friends, Anna's slender unit stretched up her arm from wrist to elbow. Eleni tore her gaze away from the fascinating keypad as a warning buzz sounded, and a d-box materialized to float in front of the ledge. It hung steadily in the air as words began to scroll across its dark surface:

WELCOME TO DRAGONVILLE! Here is the lost civilization of the dragonfolk who guard their fabulous jewelled hoards from their deadly foes, the shifters.

The shifters can be seen as misty grey outlines that can pass through solid objects and change into any shape they wish. They spit a poison that will stick to the victim. The venom is a different colour each time it hits. Five hits, and the victim will be 'dead', and out of the game. The shifters also use the hoarded gems that provide the dragons with energy and steal them whenever they can. Dragons can kill shifters, and different coloured beasts have different abilities:

Silver is an ice-dragon. Its breath freezes.

Copper breathes fire.

Emerald can pass through solid objects like the shifters.

Blue can detect shifters at a distance.

Gold is a combination of all characteristics, and is only used for third level play and upwards.

As an additional weapon, the eyes of all dragons are lasers.

Higher levels of the game will be explained when they have been reached.

Now – choose your dragon – and good luck!

The d-box vanished. In its place were four huge dragons,

one of each colour with the exception of gold, hovering in midair, as close as they could come to the ledge.

'Wow,' Eleni heard Jack mutter. 'How do we choose?'

'Now, there's a thing I forgot to mention in the instructions,' Anna said. 'This is why a fresh viewpoint is so useful.' She made a quick entry in her wrist unit. 'I'll give you the code that calls them.' She held out her wrist unit so that they could see the code on the tiny display screen. 'I suggest you store these in your own keypads for now. Later, I'll make the dragons voice-linked, so that you can just say the colour or a name out loud and they'll come. It'll save a lot of messing about.'

'I'll take silver.' Jack stepped forward and keyed the code into his unit. The gleaming silver dragon turned its head towards him, its jewelled eyes glittering at him, like rubies. It came closer, and rested its neck against the ledge so that he could scramble aboard.

'Sit astride, just where the neck joins the shoulders,' Anna said. 'Once you're on, you won't fall off.'

As Jack's dragon moved away from the ledge Rom took his place. 'Copper,' he said firmly. 'I like the idea of a beast that can breathe fire.'

That left two dragons, the emerald and the blue. Eleni hesitated. 'Why don't you take the blue dragon?' Anna suggested. 'I'll take the green if you don't mind – this one isn't quite debugged yet. I need to do a bit more work on this business of passing through solid objects. It's a lot more tricky than you'd think.'

'All right,' Eleni said. She called up the blue code and pressed the ENTER button. The great dragon turned towards her, its eyes glittering like diamonds against a hide that was the dark, rich blue of a moonlit sky. With some trepidation she scrambled off the ledge on to its warm, firm neck. Though this was only a game, the landscape was very convincing, and it seemed an awfully long way down.

As the dragon eased itself away from the cliff, she felt her heart beating fast with excitement. What an incredible feeling, to be riding a dragon. Eleni began to experiment, making her dragon swoop and turn and dive. She soon discovered that steering was easy. She only had to lean in the direction she wanted to go for the creature to change course and head that way.

'At this level, you have a few minutes to explore before the shifters come,' Anna called. 'Why not take a look into the caves?'

The caves were beautiful inside. Anna had designed the rocks to glow, so that it looked as though light was shining through chunks of thick glass coloured yellow, red, purple, and green. The floor was covered with soft sand that glittered underfoot, and piled within each cave was a hoard of sparkling crystals, each about the size of a human head. 'If your dragon seems to be slowing up or weakening, you need to bring him here to eat one of these,' Anna told them. 'If you don't remember, or if the shifters steal all the crystals, or stop you getting to them, you'll eventually fall out of the sky and it'll be game over.'

When they emerged again into the open air, Eleni glanced down over the shoulder of her dragon and saw the glint of a river, a winding silver thread that marked the bottom of the canyon. There seemed to be pale meadows on either side of the water, and the darker blur of trees beyond, but she was so high it was hard to tell. Nonetheless, she marvelled at the amount of detail that Anna had put into the game. That's why she's so successful, I suppose, she thought—

'Alert! Alert! Shifters approaching!'

Eleni realized that her own dragon was sounding the alarm.

'Look out! Behind you!' That was Rom calling.

The blue dragon made an incredible swerving, swooping turn in the air, and Eleni caught a glimpse of a hazy blur that came rocketing out of the dark caves in the moutain face. Even as she watched, the haze took on the shape of a gigantic pterodactyl. Though the form was clear and detailed, down to the leathery bat-like wings and the slender scissor-jaws like those of a crocodile, Eleni could see right through its body to the blurred, misty outlines of the crags beyond. Gripped tightly between its clawed feet, the huge winged dinosaur held a glittering red jewel, about the size of Eleni's head.

There was a snarling sound from the left, where Jack's dragon flew. Twin bolts of sizzling crimson energy lanced out of the silver dragon's eyes, converging on the point where the pterodactyl had been an instant before. A portion of rock smoked, glowed and broke off with an explosive crack.

Suddenly, another shifter appeared, oozing out of the face of the cliff, passing easily through the rock as though it was made of nothing but cobwebs. This time, the creature took the shape of a gigantic shark that swam effortlessly through the air, its gaping jaws bristling with a fearsome collection of teeth. Flying in at an angle to defend the creature that carried the jewel, it arrowed towards the dragons with startling speed.

'Split up!' Jack yelled.

Rom went right. Eleni and Jack went left – Eleni soaring upwards, Jack diving beneath the monster.

'Danger, danger!'

'Look out, Leni!'

The dragon's alarm and Rom's warning shout came at exactly the same time. Even as Eleni swerved her dragon aside there was a sharp sound like fat spitting in a frying pan, and she felt something hit her leg. She looked down to see a patch of dripping slime, coloured a luminous, lurid pink, sticking to her leg. So this was the poison. Four hits to go, and she would be down the plug.

Rom was heading for the other shifter, the pterodactyl, trying to head it off before it could escape with its prize. The shifter-shark had come around fast and was buzzing Eleni again, its pointed teeth flashing white in its cruel, wedge-shaped face. 'Shoot!' Eleni urged her dragon, and the deadly red beams shot out from its laser eyes, hitting the edge of the shark's triangular fin. The creature screamed in pain and anger. Eleni fired again, at the same time as Jack who had been coming up on it from below. The crimson lasers shot out and the shifter writhed between them, screaming, before exploding into nothingness.

Jack let out a whoop of triumph. 'Got him!' Then, as he looked past Eleni, his face fell. 'Uh-oh. Quick, Leni. Rom needs help!'

The girl turned her dragon to see Rom surrounded by four of the vast creatures, three of them carrying bright gems stolen from the dragon-caves. He was fighting bravely, his copper dragon twisting and weaving, dodging and diving, but the creature seemed to be tiring. The beams from its laser eyes were weaker and less effective than they had been. Already, Rom was spattered with blotches of the venom that stained Eleni's leg. There were three patches, one pink, one sickly yellow, and the other lurid green. Only two more hits, and he would be 'dead.'

'Come on!' Eleni shouted. 'We've got to help him!'

After that, everything happened very fast. More and more of the creatures came slithering out of the rocks, in all kinds of weird and outlandish shapes. Some came as sharks, others as jellyfish with long, trailing tentacles. There were serpents, more pterodactyls, giant wasps, and other monsters that Eleni couldn't even begin to name. She found that there was no time to think – it was all reaction and split-second timing as she dodged and swerved, fighting to get the shifters within the sights of her lasers. After a time, she began to work as a team with the others. Jack would freeze the monsters so that they hung motionless, glittering palely, caught in midair by the icy breath of his silver dragon – then Eleni would blast them to smithereens with her laser. Rom swooped down to catch the glittering crystals that the shifters dropped.

Suddenly, there were no more shifters. A buzzer sounded and a d-box appeared with a flashing message:

LEVEL 1 SUCCESSFULLY COMPLETED.
COMMENCING LEVEL 2—

There was a noise like a thunderclap, and the green dragon came hurtling straight through the face of the cliff, almost colliding with Jack's beast. The d-box vanished.

Anna pulled her dragon around to face the others. 'I'm sorry, gang, we have to break this up,' she said. 'Something has gone dreadfully wrong with the game. One of my dragons is missing.'

CHAPTER EIGHT

CODE VIOLATION RED

When Jack got up next morning he remembered that it was the day he had to travel into Wicklow Town for a day in Realworld school – and he was late, as usual. In the kitchen he found a tired, grouchy Anna making breakfast in a ferocious silence. She was doing the cooking herself instead of leaving it to the autochef, and that was usually a sign that she wanted to get something out of her system. By the sharp smell of burning that hung around the kitchen, it was doubtful whether she had succeeded. Judging from the look on her face, Jack knew better than to ask if she'd had any luck with the missing dragon. Instead, he looked for a safer subject.

'Eggs?' he said brightly. 'That'll be nice. We don't usually have a cooked breakfast.'

'I'm not usually up all night,' Anna answered shortly, sliding scrambled eggs on to a plate and thumping it down on the table in front of him. Jack picked up a piece of charred black toast and put it down again. He looked at the greasy yellow mass of his egg, speckled with brown, burnt lumps, and swallowed hard. 'Er – you didn't find the dragon then?' he asked in the politest voice he could manage.

Anna looked at his plate, blinked, and burst out laughing. She scraped the eggs into the recycler. 'I'm sorry, Jack. Shall we start again?' She turned to him with one hand on the autochef keypad. 'What would you really like for breakfast?'

'I think I'll just have cereal,' Jack said hastily.

Anna made herself some tea and sat down opposite him, and there was a brief scrimmage while the cats fought for position on her lap.

'So you didn't get anywhere with the game?' Jack asked her.

Anna shrugged. 'I just don't know what's happening. How the blazes could I lose a dragon? If that wasn't bad enough, the creature was by far and away the most advanced phace I've ever programmed. The gold dragons were very special – they had the abilities of all the other dragons put together, and what was more, they could speak.' She sighed. 'My prototype was developing in leaps and bounds – in fact I could swear it was starting to work things out for itself. It was the nearest thing to an artificial intelligence I've ever seen.'

'This probably sounds stupid,' Jack said, 'but you don't think it could have gone off somewhere on its own?'

Anna shook her head. 'No, it wasn't advanced enough yet – though don't think I haven't looked into the possibility,' she added with a wry smile. 'I can't help wondering, though, whether the game was being tampered with already. You remember I was telling you about that trouble with the shifters? They were never quite under my control, and they should have been. If they start bleeding across into other Websites, I'm in trouble. This could ruin my reputation as a designer.'

Cat couldn't remember when she'd been so happy. She supposed she would have to go back to her father some time, and she dreaded the confrontation – but that was for the future. She wouldn't think about it now. She had spent the night on the foam-form couch that she would be using during her time in the Web, and had awakened early in the morning with a tight, excited feeling in her chest as though it must be Christmas Day.

The first thing she saw when she opened her eyes was her very own Websuit, hanging beside the couch. Cat looked at it and felt her heart beat faster. Almost timidly, she reached out a hand to touch the flexible, shining material.

'Did you think you were dreaming?' The old woman's voice made her jump. Miss Aldanar was sitting in her wheelchair as though it were a throne, and she some ancient queen. Her bright, dark eyes, seemed to look right into Cat's mind.

'I never dreamed of having a suit as good as this,' Cat replied softly.

Miss Aldanar smiled. 'Well, it's about time you tried it. You'll find a bathroom of sorts on the floor below – the plumbing is all a bit makeshift here, but we manage – and Maxus will give you some breakfast. Then—' she waved a hand at the suit. 'The Web is all yours, Cat.'

When he returned in the afternoon from his Realworld lessons, Jack couldn't wait to get back into the world of the Web. He wanted to see Rom and Eleni, and chase the fade after yesterday's adventures in the dragon game. To his annoyance, they were nowhere to be found. Then he remembered that Rom, at least, lived in a different time zone in the USA, and on a schoolday, he would be in lessons right now. Eleni was probably stuck at home helping her mother again.

Jack left his sprite on Level 1 for them then entered the E&R block and found the 'Space Command' game where he had great fun shooting down enemy craft and, from time to time, being shot down himself. It seemed tame, though, to someone who had spent yesterday riding his own dragon, and, after a while, a guy called Ralph turned up and ruined things completely.

Ralph was a phreak of the worst kind – he *lived* for this game, and played all the time. Because he knew each move inside-out, no one else stood a chance when he came on the scene. Even when Jack finally let himself be wiped out, he still couldn't shake off the phreak, who, when he was in the

Web, took the appearance of an old-fashioned pilot with leather flying jacket, helmet, goggles, and a huge, curling moustache. Ralph wanted to go and chase the fade, but Jack wouldn't be seen dead in Tropicana Bay with this coggy Webhead tagging along. 'I can't,' he said quickly. 'I promised I'd meet somebody.'

When Ralph had gone to find some fellow phreaks, Jack wondered what to do next. He knew he ought to scuttle down, or risk an attack of the voms, but he didn't feel like going just yet. Why shouldn't I go and see Anna? he thought suddenly. I bet she's still in Dragonville, looking for her missing creature.

Though Anna didn't really like him to hang around too much in her games until they were finished, he knew he was welcome to visit her from time to time, and this seemed as good a time as any. He spun out of 'Space Command' and found himself back in the busy streets of the E&R Webtown. There was no way he would have been allowed into Anna's working block, but he still had yesterday's limited code that would let him into Dragonville only. Rom knew half a dozen other ways to get into the block, around the slow, low-level spiders that guarded the area against intruders, but Jack didn't want to be caught using one of *those* – not when there was no need.

As soon as he came near the block, the spiders began to close in around him, repeating: 'Restricted area Code Amber. Please leave immediately.' Jack grinned and keyed the Amber Code that Anna had given him into his wristpad. Suddenly, the spiders seemed not to see him any more, and scuttled away. Though the game wouldn't have an entrance screen in Webtown until it was finished, Jack could spin into it directly, using the game code plus Anna's access code. He entered the codes into his pad – and nothing happened.

'That's weird,' Jack muttered. He pressed the sequence of numbers again, more carefully this time, in case he had made a mistake. The keypad let out a burst of shrill electronic squeals, and a message began to flash in red on the screen:

CODE VIOLATION – RESTRICTED ACCESS ONLY.

Code violation? Jack thought. But that's impossible! What the MIP is going on?

Suddenly, he noticed that he was attracting a lot of interest. Everywhere he looked, faces turned accusingly towards the wrongdoer who had broken a restricted code. Jack writhed with embarrassment, but that wasn't the worst of it. Spiders were scurrying towards him from all directions – and these were larger, faster and far more menacing than the usual, fairly harmless guardians. Their voices were a cold, threatening buzz:

'Code Violation Red. Code Violation Red. Immediate exit compulsory.'

'Six!' Jack muttered, and pressed his scuttle button. The spiders dissolved in a sparkling cascade.

Jack ripped off his visor and heaved a sigh of relief to see the safe, familiar walls of his room around him once more. He wondered if the spiders had discovered his identity. Would they just report him to Anna, or did the Web Police become involved for a Code Red Violation? And what was the penalty? Would they take away his PAC? With an effort, he pulled himself together before his imagination ran away with him completely. 'That's just stupid,' he told himself. 'It's all a mistake – Anna must have changed the code and forgotten to tell me. I'd better let her know, so she can put things right.'

Still feeling a little shaky, he fumbled his way out of his Websuit and went to Anna's workroom. To his surprise, there was no sign of her. He found her in the kitchen, sitting at the table with her head resting in her hands. An untouched cup of tea was in front of her, and an empty microspray pack of her favourite headache killer.

Jack forgot his own problems. 'Anna? Are you all right?'

Anna jumped and looked at him as though she hardly recognized him. 'What? Oh, sorry, love, I was miles away. Today has been an absolute nightmare.' She rubbed her eyes wearily. 'I can't believe what's happened. When I punch into Dragonville some blasted idiot keeps hitting me with a Code Red Violation! I can't get into my own game!'

Anna shook her head. 'I've tried everything I can think of, but I can't get into the wretched site. I've managed to invalidate the Code Red Violation, so I can tinker around now without being buried in spiders every time I make a move, but that's all.' She sighed. 'I'll tell you something, though. Whoever set up that Violation was a master. It took half the day to track down the new programming, and the other half to undo it.'

'But who would want to seal off an unfinished game?' Jack wondered. 'Do you think it could be something to do with the disappearance of the other sites, like Menagerie?'

'There could well be a connection,' Anna admitted. 'In any case, the culprit may be someone who wants to complete my game their own way, and that's what really worries me.' Anna frowned. 'Dragonville is registered in my name, so if anything goes wrong, I'm legally responsible.'

CHAPTER NINE

CAT AND GARGOYLE

A day in Realworld school meant Realworld homework, but Jack was too busy puzzling over the mystery to concentrate on his studies that evening. Eventually he gave it up as a bad job, spun out of the Education block and back to Level 1. Maybe he could find Rom and Eleni . . . But he didn't, and his sprite was just where he'd left it. Instead, the first person he saw was the last person he'd expected. To his surprise, a slender girl with short dark hair and wide, smiling green eyes came up to him and held out a hand. 'I found your sprite.' She bit her lip and looked away from him. 'I'm sorry I lost my temper the other day,' she said. 'Will you forgive me?'

It wasn't! It couldn't be—

'Jack?' she said. 'It's me, Cat.'

'But—' At last Jack found his voice. 'But you *never* come into the Web as a human.'

Cat shrugged. 'That was then. This is now. Things have changed for me, Jack.' A small frown appeared on her pretty face. 'Don't you like it?'

'I love it,' he said hastily – and it was true. The funny thing was, her little pointed face still looked very cat-like, with those high cheekbones and huge green eyes. Jack found himself wondering if the human form she was using now was anything like her Realworld appearance.

Suddenly, it seemed very important to get to the bottom of the mystery that was Cat. 'What about going to Tropicana

Bay?' Jack suggested. 'I can leave my sprite for—' He clapped his hand to his forehead. 'I nearly forgot! I still have *your* sprite, the one that Anna made for you, if you want it, that is.'

Cat's face broke into an enormous smile. 'Oh, Jack, I would love it! I'm really sorry about what I said. I didn't mean it. I was just having a bad day.'

'It doesn't matter,' Jack said, marvelling at the change in her. It seemed that the old sulky, sharp-voiced Cat had gone – he hoped, for ever. This new version was much nicer.

From his own wrist unit, Jack accessed the coding for Cat's sprite. He held the wristpad out so that she could see the series of numbers. 'Key in this code,' he told her, 'and then your PAC.' Cat punched the two series of numbers into her wristpad, and a tiny figure sprang into existence on her outstretched hand.

'Oh, yuk!' Jack made a face.

'Jack, how can you say that? He's *perfect*!' Cat's face was alight with pleasure.

That Cat! He would never understand her. Jack looked again at the little gargoyle with its black, furry body, its long, clawed, spidery fingers and its batlike wings. Its wrinkled face was also like that of a bat, with an upturned snout, long white fangs and sharply pointed ears. It was absolutely hideous, he thought. As he put his head closer for a better look, it squinted its glittering red eyes at him and made a rude gesture.

Cat crowed with laughter. 'Oh, Jack, it's wonderful! It's the most amazingly venomous thing I've ever seen! How does Anna do it? How did she know just exactly what I'd like?'

Jack shrugged. 'There's no accounting for taste, but I'm glad you like it. Now, if you've finished admiring the horrible creature, how about heading off to Tropicana Bay?'

Cat stuck her tongue out at him. 'He's *not* horrible and I

don't think I'll ever finish admiring him. Tropicana Bay sounds fine.'

When Cat finally emerged from the Web, she was amazed to see that the windows of the cathedral tower were already dark. She had spent the last two days exploring the Web – by far the longest time she had ever spent there – apart from her sleep-time and several hour-long breaks to stave off the voms. She had loved every moment. It was so different having unlimited access to the Web. Her meeting with Jack tonight had been the best part, though. It made such a difference not to have to bother about the time ticking away.

Miss Aldanar was looking at her with eyes that burned bright in her hawk-like face. 'Well? Did you have a good time, my dear?'

'It was eight!' Cat said enthusiastically, then remembered that she was talking to an old woman. 'That is, it was marvellous.'

Miss Aldanar laughed. 'It's all right, I know what eight means. Why, I might even have made up the word myself. I've invented so many things in my time, it's difficult to remember them all,' she added quietly.

Cat was surprised when the old woman suggested that they might spend some time in the Web together. 'There's so much I can show you,' she said. 'I can get you into sites where you wouldn't normally be allowed to go.'

Cat was reluctant. She had been planning to meet Jack again tomorrow, and was looking forward to it. But she owed Miss Aldanar so much. She wouldn't have any of this had it not been for the old lady's kindness. It wouldn't hurt her to spare a few hours. Miss Aldanar, at her age, could hardly be expected to spend too long in the Web. Cat could always leave her new sprite for Jack, and meet him later. It would give her a chance to try the little creature out.

Unfortunately, Cat's conscience, having bothered her

once, decided to rear its ugly head again. Dad would be ever so worried about her by now, and those dratted little eggs would be missing their big sister. Though she didn't want to go back home – at least not yet – something would have to be done.

'Miss Aldanar?' she said tentatively. 'Do you think we ought to find some way of letting Dad know I'm all right?' For the first time, it struck her as peculiar that a grown-up could have been so unconcerned about such an important detail.

The old woman frowned. 'I suppose it would be wise, my dear, but we must think very carefully about what we'll tell him. Do you really want to go home, Cat? I thought you were unhappy there.'

Cat felt a stab of alarm. 'No, no,' she said quickly. 'If I go back he'll never let me come here again. He must never be allowed to find out about this place. I just, well, he'll be worrying, that's all,' she finished lamely.

Miss Aldanar's frown changed to a smile. 'You're right of course. We mustn't alarm him unduly. Why don't we spend a pleasant day together tomorrow as we planned, and in the meantime I'll try to think of a way to reassure your father. How does that sound?'

'That would be wonderful,' Cat said gratefully. She was hugely relieved. Trust Miss Aldanar to know what to do. The old lady was incredibly kind to her!

Next morning, Miss Aldanar was all briskness. 'Now, it'll take a while for Maxus to help me get into my suit, so why don't you go on ahead? I'll meet you on Level 1 as soon as I'm ready. You'll know me by my ring.'

'OK,' Cat nodded. 'I'll see you in a little while.' Maybe, if she was quick, she would run into Jack while she was waiting. She hurried off to get into her Websuit, and within minutes, was lost in the world of the Web.

When Cat was safely out of Realworld, the old woman

turned to the hulking figure of Maxus. 'Right. Pay attention. First, I want you to come with me to Dragonville. Now we've finally discovered how to encode stolen information in those energy crystals the dragons collect, we must set that part of our plan in action. Once we've loosed the dragons and the shifters, I want to concentrate on the girl. I daren't waste any more time, Maxus. We're going to take her today.'

The big man frowned. 'So soon?' he asked sadly.

The old woman's eyes flashed with anger. 'Imbecile! Don't go soft on me now, or I'll make you wish you had never been born! We must act before she has a chance to contact her family. Do you *understand*?'

Maxus sighed. 'Yes, madam. I won't fail you, I know how important this is. I'll do my part. It's just—'

'I know, you great fool,' the old woman said softly. 'But I'm dying, Maxus. Don't you see, I have no choice?'

The big man looked away from her. 'I know, madam. You've always been so good to me since you took me off the streets when I was a child. I don't want to lose you.'

The ghost of a smile crossed the old woman's bony face. 'Dear Maxus,' she said softly. 'What would I do without you?' She took a deep breath. 'Now, are you quite clear about what you have to do? First we release the dragons and the shifters. Then, as soon as I take the child into the labyrinth, you spin back here and swap over the connections on the two Websuits.' She pointed to the white box into which both sets of Websuit cables vanished. 'When you take away the girl's keypad she'll be safely trapped in the Web – and when I come back to Realworld, I will find myself in a new, healthy young body.'

CHAPTER TEN

DRAGON RAID

Though autumn was on its way, it was easily still warm enough for Eleni's family to eat breakfast outside on the terrace overlooking the sparkling bay where the far horizon was hazy in the silvery morning light. In a hurry to get into the Web, she gulped down her breakfast, excused herself hastily and left the table while the rest of her family was still eating.

'Are lessons so interesting that you have to rush away to them?' the voice of her father floated after her. Eleni felt her face grow warm with guilt. As he clearly suspected, her destination this morning was *not* the Education block – at least not entirely. 'I have to hurry, Papa,' she called back over her shoulder. 'I have a lot to do today.' Well, that was true, at any rate.

Yesterday, Eleni reflected as she climbed into her Websuit, had been one of those awful days when nothing had gone right. It had been a school day, but after the excitement of the day before, her thoughts had been all over the place, and she hadn't done as well as usual. She had been late getting home from Corfu Town, late with her usual chores, then Mama, it seemed, had gone out of her way to find a hundred other irksome little jobs for her to do, until it had been too late to enter the Web at all.

This morning would be different, though, Eleni promised herself. She was determined to catch Jack. She knew he'd be heading for the Education block to catch up on the homework from yesterday's class. Maybe they could get together, instead, and chase the fade at last. Settling herself comfortably on her foam form couch, she pulled down her visor and heaved a sigh of relief as Level 1 sprang into life around her.

Education was busy that morning, with crowds of students popping in and out of the various blocks. Eleni thought about trying out her sprite for the first time, but as it turned out, there was no need. She was loitering near the entry area, keying in Jack's code for the sprite, when he spun in. 'Leni!' he cried. 'Am I glad to see you! All sorts of things have been happening. You'll never guess—'

Taking her arm, he pulled her back towards the entry point. 'Where can we talk?' he muttered. 'Everywhere's too busy at this time of day.'

'What about—' The words were swept out of Eleni's mouth by the screech of an alarm klaxon, followed by the sound of a deafening roar. A glittering green dragon burst out of one of the buildings in the Education block, clutching a cluster of sparkling cyrstals in its talons. Screaming people threw themselves to the ground. Others scattered left and right like scurrying ants as the dragon banked dangerously low across the Webtown. With another ear-splitting bellow, it skirted the official entry point and vanished through the wall.

Eleni and Jack looked at one another, horrified. Before they even had time to collect their thoughts, the whole of the area was suddenly aswarm with spiders, most of which looked considerably bigger, darker and meaner than the usual inoffensive little security patrollers. Eleni shuddered as a great, dark-green hairy creature about the size of a small pony approached them.

'*Identify yourselves,*' it said. '*State destination and personal access codes.*'

One at a time, Jack and Eleni gave their PACs to the spider. '*Destination?*' it demanded again.

'Secondary area,' Jack said hastily, 'and we're late.' Grabbing Eleni's hand, he pulled her quickly away, continuing to tug her as they ran together down the nearest strand, until they were well out of sight of the spiders.

When they finally came to a halt, Eleni looked at Jack. 'What's going on?' she said. 'That was one of Anna's dragons from the game!'

'The green one,' Jack said grimly. 'The one that goes through walls. So that was what they were up to!'

'Who?'

'Whoever blocked off the access to Dragonville yesterday. Look, there are spiders here, too. Keep walking, as if we're going somewhere, and I'll tell you about it.'

Eleni listened in astonishment as Jack told her what had happened when he had tried to return to Dragonville, and how Anna herself was now locked out of her own game. 'But that's terrible,' she said. 'Who could have done such a thing? And why?'

'My guess is—' Jack's words were cut off abruptly. Walking aimlessly, they had strayed into the Tertiary Area, with its peaceful green lawns lined with university blocks. Even as Jack spoke, a shadowy figure oozed through the wall of a nearby research facility – the misty figure of a horned demon, its clawed hands full of sparkling crystals. Cackling evilly, it vanished in a flash of flame, even as alarm bells began to ring within the block. Jack groaned. 'The shifters are loose too, Eleni. We're down the plug now and no mistake.'

What in the world is happening? Cat thought, as she entered Level 1. Where did all these enormous spiders come from? Well, if there had been some kind of trouble, she had best get herself out of here. She would just leave her sprite for Jack.

Cat keyed the sprite code on her wrist unit and smiled with delight as the little black imp popped into existence on the palm of her hand, baring its fangs at her in a wicked grin. This was much better than Leni's coggy fairy. Working quickly, she keyed Jack's PAC and, since she didn't know where Miss Aldanar would be taking her, she programmed the sprite for a 'follow me', the function that would enable it to track her wherever she went within the Web. Spreading its batlike wings, the sprite flew off to wait for Jack.

Cat got another unpleasant surprise when she spun into the E&R Webtown. The normally-crowded streets were close to deserted, except for more spiders than she had ever seen in her life. *It's me they're after!* was the first panic-stricken thought that flashed through the Cat's head. Don't be such a gag, she told herself firmly. All these nasty-looking, high-level spiders for one runaway girl?

Nevertheless, in this all-too-public place, Cat felt horribly exposed wearing her human form and her own face. Though she could think of no one, apart from her friends, who might recognize her, the crowds of spiders made her very nervous. Besides, if her father had told the police she was missing, her description just might have been circulated.

Clumsy with haste, Cat fumbled for her wrist unit. The next minute, the dark-haired, human girl with the pointed face had vanished, and in its place stood a small grey tabby cat, with a black-ringed tail that twitched uneasily back and forth. With a quick glance right and left, Cat darted down a narrow access between two blocks where she could hope-fully stay out of sight and still keep an eye on the entry point. She wished Miss Aldanar would hurry up and arrive. She had a feeling that the formidable old woman would be more than a match for any spider.

When Miss Aldanar finally did come, it was not from the direction Cat had anticipated, and not in a guise she had expected. In fact, the woman could only be recognized by her ring with its glittering red stone. Her dark hair streamed out behind her like bonfire smoke, lit with flashes of red-gold light that might have been flame. In her skintight suit of shining silver, and the expressionless silver mask that gave her face a mantis-like appearance, she truly looked like the sorceress of Cat's imagination.

Greatly relieved, the Cat rushed out to meet her, forgetting, in her hurry, that Miss Aldanar would not be able to recognize *her*. To her astonishment, however, the woman had no difficulty at all. 'Ah, there you are.' The sorceress said briskly. 'I like your shape, my dear. It takes great talent to move so comfortably in the guise of an animal. Now I know why you call yourself Cat – or is it the other way around? Did the shape come from the name?'

At that moment a huge, spiky black spider came scuttling up to them, and Cat shrank nervously away from the formidable creature.

'Immediate identity required,' it demanded.

'State destination and personal access codes.'

Miss Aldanar's silver mask glittered coldly. 'Sorceress,' she snapped, much to Cat's delighted surprise. 'Code Triple-platinum – security override.'

Abruptly, the spider seemed to shrink in on itself.

'Apologies, Madam – override in place.' Quickly, it scuttled away.

'Come along,' Miss Aldanar told the astounded Cat, looking as cool as if she ate advanced-level spiders for breakfast. 'We don't have all day. Would you mind going back to your usual shape, my dear? I like the cat, but I'm old-fashioned enough to feel easier talking to a human being. Now, hold out your arm, and let me see your wrist unit.'

When the Cat was human once more, the silver-masked woman took her arm and began to tap a code into her keypad. 'Excuse me, Cat,' she apologized, 'but these are adult-only codes, and I can't reveal them to you.'

As the sorceress finished entering the codes, there was a flash of Blue and Tone, and the Cat found herself standing, with the silver woman, on a high cliff overlooking a jagged mountain range of reddish stone. Far below, in the purple shadows of a canyon, dragons flew and played. Miss Aldanar turned to her. 'What do you think of it, my dear? Welcome to Dragonville.'

The world seemed to stand still around the Cat. 'Dragonville?' she blurted without thinking. 'But that's an Anna Lucas game.'

The cold metallic mask turned slowly towards the girl. Cat realized, with a chill, that though its surface appeared to be gleaming silver, it reflected nothing. 'And who's to say that *I* am not Anna Lucas?' the sorceress asked in a voice made of claws and steel.

Suddenly, the Cat realized that something was dangerously wrong. Why had this woman lied to her? Just who was she, anyway? Had Cat been wrong to trust her?

CHAPTER ELEVEN

A FAMILIAR FACE

Cat's first instinct was to hit her scuttle button and get out of there as fast as she could, but the curiosity that went with her name got the better of her. Her new friend was up to something, but Miss Aldanar had never attempted to harm her, after all. In fact, she had shown Cat nothing but kindness. Besides, Cat told herself, if this silver woman was doing anything bad to Anna's game, then surely it would be better to find out about it so that the designer could be warned?

Caught in a tangle of loyalties, Cat hesitated. Then it was too late.

'Well, Cat,' Miss Aldanar smiled. 'How would you like to ride a dragon?'

That settled it.

Riding one of the great winged creatures was an incredible experience. Cat's flame-breathing copper dragon shone red-gold like a bright new coin in the alien sunlight, and looked every bit as splendid as the sorceress's silver mount. But, while Miss Aldanar's flight was steady, level and businesslike, Cat and her dragon were darting all over the sky, diving, swooping, banking and swerving like a great red kite gone mad.

After a while, the sorceress called them to order. 'Come along now, Cat, I have something to show you.'

Reluctantly, Cat guided her dragon to the side of the silver beast. 'But we were having so much fun,' she protested.

'Be still,' Miss Aldanar snapped coldly, 'and do as you're told. Remember how lucky you are to be here at all.'

Cat fell sulkily into position behind the silver dragon, deciding not to push her luck. Miss Aldanar could be very kind, but obviously it wasn't wise to cross her. They flew on for a time in silence, until Cat began to get bored with looking at mountains and canyons, cliffs and crags. Why did I say I'd come with the old battleaxe, she thought gloomily. I could be with Jack right now, having some fun. We could— *What the MIP is that?*

Cat's first thought was of the famous 'face' on Mars, the mysterious feature that the Olympus Mission would soon be investigating once and for all. The image below her was many kilometres long and filled the floor of the valley below. It had the contours of a gigantic face carved into the soft red rock, and the features were unmistakably those of a young Miss Aldanar, the face that was now hidden behind the expressionless silver mask.

The silver dragon was circling above the proud and lovely face, losing height as it spiralled down. A shiver went through Cat – excitement or fear, she was no longer sure. If this was Anna's game, then how had this face come to be here? Sending her own mount into a dive, she caught up quickly with Miss Aldanar. 'Are we going down *there*?' she yelled. 'Is it really you?'

The Sorceress glanced back at her. 'Trust me,' she said in a gentle voice, 'I have something to show you.'

Swallowing her doubts, Cat followed the silver woman down. Indeed, it seemed impossible now to disobey her. Down, down, they went, towards the gigantic mouth, that was open in an enigmatic half-smile. *Oh, no.* Cat thought. *Oh, please, surely not in there—* As they neared the massive opening, she could see a long dark tunnel winding away into the depths of the earth. Then they were inside, Miss Aldanar's silver dragon glimmering faintly like a ghost in the dim light as it headed for the tunnel.

With a hideous grinding noise, the mouth snapped shut behind the Cat. She screamed in panic as the darkness swallowed her, and groped frantically for her scuttle button, suddenly desperate to escape. Terror squeezed her heart in an icy fist. She was alone in the dark, and her keypad was gone!

In the Education block, the rumours were flying thick and fast. Despite the efforts of the spiders to keep order, the normal business of the day had ground to a halt. Jack and Eleni split up for a while and wandered through the strands, mingling with the crowds of people who were also collecting and passing on the growing number of stories. After an hour, they met back at the prearranged place – the half-completed castle in their rented E&R design space – to compare notes.

They sat on the battlements, swinging their legs while they shared what they had discovered. It appeared that data on a wide range of subjects was being stolen throughout the Web. Among all sorts of weird and wonderful stuff, the following stood out:

The Cryogenics Department of the university had lost virtually-encoded samples and the results of their latest experiments on cold sleep in which they were working to preserve living bodies by freezing them.

Bigene Industrie, who had been working on an advanced project to grow limbs and organs for transplant, had also lost top-secret experimental data.

Helnen Robotics, a company at the cutting edge of the development of Artificial Intelligence, were frantically denying that they had lost *anything* – and everyone knew what that meant.

A whole screed of varied data from the Olympus Mission, for goodness' sake, had been spirited away in mid-transmission.

Jack frowned when Eleni told him the last one. 'What on

earth is going on?' he muttered. 'Who can be doing this? Why do they want all this stuff – and what are they doing with Anna's game?'

'I think you ought to talk to her,' Eleni suggested. 'Why not send your sprite for her?'

Jack shook his head. 'I would, but she isn't in the Web this morning. She was up all night trying to get into Dragonville, and I left her fast asleep when I spun in earlier.'

'Go back, then,' Eleni urged him. 'Spin out and talk to her, Jack. These are her creatures, running amok in the Web and stealing everything in site. What if they blame her? She's got to be warned!'

Jack looked at her in horror. 'You're right. I never thought of that. Listen, Leni, I'll come back and meet you at Tropicana Bay as soon as I can.'

'And while you're gone, I'll try to find Rom,' Eleni added. 'If anyone can get a handle on this mystery, he can.'

'Good idea. And while you're at it, keep a lookout for the Cat. I promised I'd meet her today, and what with everything that's been happening I clean forgot!'

'I will. See you later, Jack.' Then Eleni vanished as Jack hit his scuttle button and left the Web.

Jack shed his Websuit quickly, and threw it down on the couch a little too hard. It slithered over the edge and disappeared between couch and wall. Jack muttered a word he wasn't supposed to know, but left the suit where it lay. He could come back for it in a minute, but first he needed to find Anna.

She was still in her room, fast asleep, the cats, three slumbering balls of fur, curled up with her on the quilt. 'Anna,' Jack called, shaking her shoulder. 'Anna! Wake up!'

'Wha—' Anna rolled over, spilling indignant cats left and right. Opening a bleary eye she blinked up at Jack. 'What's wrong?'

'Everything,' said Jack. 'Wake up, Anna, quick! Something

terrible has happened.' Wasting no time, he told her what
he and Leni had witnessed that morning in the Education
block.

'My *dragons* are loose?' Anna stopped rubbing her eyes,
leaped out of bed and made a dash for the kitchen. She
grabbed a coffee bulb from the autochef and perched up on
a high stool, her sleepy gaze suddenly sharp and intent. 'All
right, Jack, just tell me again, slowly and clearly. From the
beginning.'

When Jack had finished telling her what had been happening that morning, Anna simply sat there a moment,
looking stunned, her brows knitted together in a frown.
Then she leaped from the stool, throwing the bulb in the
general direction of the recycler. 'I'd better go and see—'
She fell silent and stopped as though she had been turned
to stone, staring out of the window that looked right out
across the valley and the sweeping hills beyond. Three
white cars were speeding up the valley road, coming very
fast.

Abruptly, Anna came back to life. 'Police!' she gasped.
'Jack, get out of here. I don't want you involved in this. If
they don't arrest me, come back. If they do— Go home –
call your mum and tell her. Take the cats with you.' Already
she was bundling him out of the back door, scooping up
cats and throwing them out after him. Startled by such
abrupt treatment, they went streaking away up the garden
and into the woodland beyond. Jack ran after them as
the sound of the approaching sirens grew louder and
louder.

'Call your mum!' Anna yelled after Jack. 'Get into the
woods, quick! Don't let them see you!' Behind him, the door
slammed shut.

The woods were dense with a low-level tangle of unseen
roots, and brambles that caught in Jack's clothing and tore
at his unprotected skin. Cursing under his breath, he
mopped at the blood from a deep, stinging scratch across his

face, dangerously close to his eye. When you had been spending so much time in the Web, you sometimes forgot how things in Realworld could hurt and damage you.

Keeping under the cover of the trees, Jack scrambled along the hillside until he came to a place where he could see the front of Anna's house. Hidden in the bushes, he watched the door. The sleek police cars, each with a luminous yellow stripe along its sides, were parked in the lane in front of the house. Were they questioning Anna in there? Were they giving her a hard time? Jack, unable to do anything but watch and wait, had never felt so cold, so lonely, and so helpless. It was different in the Web, he thought bitterly. There, no one was bigger or stronger than himself. He was the equal of his surroundings, and could almost always find a way to make things work the way he wanted. Between them, he and Rom knew fifty ways to outwit a spider, but out here in Realworld he was helpless against the power and strength of these officers of the law. It was not a pleasant feeling.

Just when Jack was about ready to explode with impatience, the front door opened, and Anna walked out, flanked by three officers, two women and a man. Anna was ushered into the first car, and as Jack watched, his skin prickling with horror, its engine started and with a snarl of its motors, it shot away down the valley. They had arrested Anna!

At that moment, two other officers came out of the house with armloads of Anna's equipment. With a chill, Jack recognized her Websuit. They began loading everything into the second vehicle. Eventually, they too sped away, leaving two men behind with the last car, clearly guarding the house. I wonder why, Jack thought. Maybe they think she has an accomplice, or something.

Then the realization hit him. *But she does, you idiot. You!* he told himself. And he was the only one who could help her now. He must warn the others what had happened right away. If they could only find a way to break into the game, maybe— A second shock hit him. In the rush to escape, he had left his Websuit in Anna's house!

CHAPTER TWELVE

NIGHT STALK

'Are you *sure* you'll be all right until tomorrow?' On the vidscreen, his mother was frowning. 'There's just no way I can get back until then.'

'Mum, of course I'll be all right,' Jack sighed. 'I know how to work the thermostat and the autochef, and I'll be sure to lock up properly. What could go wrong?'

'You're right, love. I'm sorry. I'll be back tomorrow afternoon, OK? I'll see you then.'

'Bye, Mum.' Jack snapped the screen off with a sigh of relief. Well, that was one ordeal over. Why did parents go ballistic every time the slightest little thing went wrong? It didn't help in the least. Not, Jack thought, that this was a little thing. He glanced out of the window for about the twentieth time. It's getting dark at last, he thought. His insides knotted in a queer mixture of relief and nervousness. Police or no police, he was going back to Anna's house to get his Websuit – if they hadn't already taken it away.

Jack went into his bedroom for his jacket and found the cats asleep on his bed, full of tuna. He was relieved that they seemed to have settled. He'd had an awful time hunting for them in the woods, afraid to call too loud in case the police should hear him. He left them sleeping, slipped his torch into his jacket pocket, and rummaged in the drawer of the hall table until he found the spare key for Anna's back door, the one she always left with them for emergencies. Well, this was an emergency and no mistake, he thought, as he slipped out of the house and crept away into the night.

They had turned on the outside lights at Anna's house. Jack could see the glow at the end of the lane and was grateful for it. It gave him something to aim for in this pitch-dark night, though the shadows of the high hedge kept the light from the uneven ground of the track under his feet. Jack hadn't even dared attempt the tangled woods in darkness. Even the rough, rutted surface of the lane had been too much for him, for he had been unable to use the torch in case the police were watching. To his dismay, it was taking him ages to stumble to the end of a track that he could run along in two minutes in the daylight.

When he rounded the corner at the bottom of the lane, Jack almost fell over the long nose of the car, parked at the bottom of Anna's drive. Without thinking, he threw himself to one side and dived into the hedge, adding more scratches to his collection. He lay there, motionless in the shadows, scarcely daring to breathe. Out of the corner of his eye, he had caught a glimpse of a dark silhouette behind the streamlined windshield of the vehicle. The police were inside, watching the house from the lane!

This was an unexpected development. Somehow, Jack had pictured the officers sitting in Anna's kitchen, laughing and drinking her coffee, but clearly, even though she had been arrested and they had seized her equipment, they were not allowed to make free with her house. Or was it a trap? Were they just lying in wait to see if anyone came by? Well, they wouldn't see him – not if he could help it. Anna was always complaining about dogs getting through the holes in her hedge, but Jack was grateful now. He groped in the darkness until he found a gap, and crawled through.

Anna's garden was a patchwork of brilliant light and knife-edged shadow. Worming his way between the patches of thick shade, he managed to get close to the building without breaking cover. Once he reached the back of the house he would be out of sight of the police, but first he would have to get across the lawn at the side, lit bright as a football stadium by lights designed to deter burglars. There was no way round it. If he wanted his Websuit back, Jack was going to have to cross that stretch of open ground, in full view of the men in the car.

Crouched under a bush, Jack waited, watching the faces of the two policemen, pale and distinct in the glare of the security lights. Though he could see their lips moving as they talked, they never allowed their attention to wander from the house for even a moment. Jack waited and waited, all the time growing colder. Already, his feet and fingers and the tip of his nose were numb and aching. That never happened in the Web, either, he thought ruefully. To make matters worse, the shrub was the sort with thorns, and the long spines were sticking painfully into his back.

Endless minutes went by until, at last, Jack was jerked out of a daydream by a sudden movement in the vehicle. At last, something was happening! One of the men rummaged down on the floor and came up with a thermal container of coffee. As he opened it, a thread of the rich scent came drifting through the car window. Jack tensed himself, getting ready to move. This could be his only chance! The second officer turned towards the first, holding out a cup while the other poured. Jack was up and away like a rabbit, darting across the open lawn.

He had forgotten his numb feet. Staggering and stumbling, he felt himself beginning to fall. With a desperate, wrenching effort, he hurled himself forward, diving towards the corner of the house. Jack hit the ground hard and rolled under the wooden bench that stood against the wall. He was out of sight now – but had they spotted him? He lay there unmoving, scarcely daring to breathe, listening for any trace of a sound from the police car while pins and needles chased furiously up his legs.

After a few minutes, Jack decided he must be safe. Keeping low, he crept along beside the wall until he reached the back door. Luckily, because he fed the cats so often in Anna's absence, the burglar alarm was set to recognize his voice. 'It's me, Jack,' he said softly into the little brown box set into the wall, then he slipped the keycard into the slot, opened the back door just a crack, and slipped inside.

Now, at last, the torch came in handy. Shielding the end with his hand so that only a soft red glow escaped between his fingers, Jack crept through the kitchen and up the shadowed staircase to the spare room. Thrusting his hand down the side of the couch, he breathed a sigh of relief. The suit was there! Laying down the torch, he fished the special carrying bag from under the couch, rolled up the Websuit and stowed it carefully inside. Just as he was zipping the bag, his hand caught the torch that was lying on the couch. It fell to the floor with a clatter, and switched itself on.

With a groan of dismay, Jack dived on top of the torch to muffle the light and fumbled frantically for the switch. A moment's silence followed, then he heard the double slam of the police car's doors, murmuring voices growing louder, and the crunch of booted feet on the gravelled path. The front door banged open and footsteps came thundering up the stairs. The two policemen burst into the spare room – and stopped. The room was empty.

It took a moment for one of the officers to realize that the blind was down, covering the window, as it had not been when they had seen the light shine out. Lifting a corner, he saw the open window and the roof of the porch below. The lane and the garden beyond were completely empty. There was no one in sight.

Jack rubbed his skinned knees and the shoulder that he'd bruised in his headlong slide from the sloping porch roof. In that first, stunned moment when he'd crashed to the ground, he had noticed the front door, still open. In an instant he had slipped back into the house and through the hall to hide under the bench in the kitchen. Now, crouched panting in the darkness, he heard footsteps thundering back downstairs.

'He must be in the lane,' one of them said.

'He can't get far,' the other replied. 'The car's heat-tracer will soon pick him up.' After a few minutes, Jack heard the engine start, and the crunch of gravel as the car pulled away.

Jack almost fell asleep during the time the aircar was cruising up and down the lane. He stayed where he was, knowing there was enough gadgetry in the kitchen to disguise *his* body heat from the tracer. It was hard to be patient. There came a point when he was convinced that the police had given up and gone back to Dublin for good. Just as he was about to leave his hiding-place, however, he heard a throb of motors, and then silence again as the car stopped outside. That was what he had been waiting for. In a flash, Jack was out of the back door, across the garden and into the woods. Glancing back one last time through a screen of bushes, he saw the lights go on in the house, as the policemen finally thought to search there.

When Jack got home, scratched, scraped, muddy but triumphant, he didn't waste any time. He dialled a soy-burger from the autochef, and had a quick wash between bites, so as not to get mud in his Websuit. Carefully, he unfolded the precious suit from its carrying bag and plugged it into the terminal in his room. At last, he was ready to go. He only hoped the others would still be there.

As Jack spun into Level 1, he was immediately pounced upon by a tiny, bat-winged imp that flew round his head, chattering. The Cat had left her sprite for him. I'd better find her quickly, he thought. She should be in on this. He caught hold of the sprite, knowing it was keyed to Cat's wrist unit, and would take him to her automatically. But, after the Blue and Tone had cleared, he found himself, to his puzzlement, in E&R Webtown, outside Anna's work block, with about twenty menacing spiders heading his way.

CHAPTER THIRTEEN

THE DRAGON QUEEN

The dragon was a dream – or perhaps a nightmare – brought to life. It was so huge that its outstretched wings filled the immense chamber from floor to ceiling, and its head towered so high that Cat had to bend backwards to look at it. Its scales were a burnished gold that dazzled where they caught the light that shot down, in a single slender beam like a spotlight, from some hidden place above. From the top of its hoard, a vast pile of multicoloured crystals, it gazed down at her with glittering, cold eyes that held a merciless intelligence. Cat couldn't run. The eyes transfixed her, holding her in place. They reminded her of something. Into Cat's mind flashed an image of Miss Aldanar's cold, dark eyes, glittering behind the silver mask.

Miss Aldanar and her silver dragon had disappeared about the same time as Cat's wrist unit. The other dragon – the one who'd brought her here – had dumped her from its back and disappeared. Cat knew there could be no escape. She would never be able to find her way back through the weird maze of chambers that had finally led to this vast and gloomy room, with its echoing spaces and its walls and ceiling lost in the crowding shadows.

Cat took a hasty step backwards. *This is the Web*, she told herself. *Nothing can harm me – this thing can't eat me.* Somehow, it was hard to convince herself. *Don't let it be hungry – please.*

The dragon cocked its great head and looked at her with

calm curiosity, rather, Cat thought, as a bird would eye a beetle before it pounced. Cat saw the enormous teeth, each as long as her arm, and shuddered. With a noise like someone crumpling a sheet of paper ten miles wide, the dragon shuddered its gigantic wings. 'So,' it said in a dry, clear voice.

Cat gasped. 'Miss Aldanar!'

'As you say.'

'Why—' Cat tried to keep the quaver out of her voice, and failed. 'Why have you brought me here? I don't like it. Can we go now, please?'

The doors flew open, slamming back against the wall with a hollow booming sound. Maxus stood there, his expression grim. 'Madam, it's done,' he said quietly.

The dragon looked down at Cat with its pitiless, inhuman gaze. 'Child,' it said, 'you won't be going anywhere. You'll stay here in the Web with me for ever.'

'No!' Cat shrieked. 'I can't stay here!' Then she was running, back towards the great bronze doors that were the only entrance to the chamber. Before she could reach them, shifters came oozing through the walls wearing all sorts of hideous shapes: mosquitoes and maggots, giant wasps and scorpions, sharks and squid. And others were like escapees from every horror vid that Cat had ever seen. There were ghosts and banshees, zombies dropping a trail of rotten flesh, armies of grinning skeletons, hollow-eyed mummies trailing their stained bandages, and disembodied heads with gnashing teeth.

From behind Cat came the dry, cold voice of the dragon. 'Never think that you can't die here,' it said in a voice like ice and steel. 'I promise you, you can.'

'What can have gone wrong?' Eleni asked Rom anxiously. 'Do you think something has happened?'

Hours had passed since Jack had promised to meet the others at Tropicana Bay. Eleni and Rom had sat at the tables under the trees and listened to people talking about the thefts, which apparently were still taking place. They had swum several times with the dolphins in the silver sea, and each of them in turn had taken an hour's break out of the Web to stave off the voms. Still, Jack had not come. Rom shrugged. 'If Jack promised to come, he'll come, sooner or later. Something must have held him up, that's all.'

It was all right for Rom to be so cool, Eleni thought with a flash of resentment. It wasn't late at night where he lived, and *his* mother didn't seem obsessed with the notion that young people needed their sleep. Mama isn't pleased with me already, she thought, because I said I couldn't help her tonight. If she comes in and catches me in the Web when I ought to be in bed, there'll be no end of trouble, but there's no way I'm leaving now.

When Eleni had just about given up hope, Jack finally appeared. He had barely spun in before he was calling out to them. 'They've arrested Anna!'

Eleni and Rom looked at each other in horror as Jack told them what had happened. 'We can't let them do this,' Eleni said. 'We've got to help her!'

'We've got to get into the game,' Rom said. 'Everything depends on that. If we can only find out who's really doing this, and take the police some proof—'

'Anna herself couldn't get into it,' Jack said grimly, 'but someone else has. I found the Cat's sprite waiting, and that's where it led me, except I couldn't get into Dragonville, of course. I was well and truly spidered off. But the Cat is in there, for sure, so how did *she* do it?'

'And did she mean to?' Rom added quietly, 'or is she in trouble?'

I suppose the game will close for ever, like Dreamcastle, Eleni was thinking. What a shame. It was so wonderful to ride a dragon. Ride a dragon! She leaped to her feet. 'Jack, Rom, I've got the answer! I know how to get us into the game!'

'Eleni, are you *sure* this will work?' Rom said. 'We've been waiting here for ages.'

'Have you a better idea?' Eleni snapped. 'Education must be the best place. As soon as the dragon appears again.'

'*If* it appears.'

'There!' Jack shouted. In a flash of green, the dragon came bursting through one of the Tertiary research buildings, a single crystal clasped between its jaws. From his wrist unit, Jack called up Anna's code that summoned the creatures. For a second the dragon seemed to hesitate in midair, then it changed its course and came to land beside them.

There was pandemonium. From nowhere, a horde of spiders appeared. Everywhere, people were running – some towards the dragon, others away. Eleni and the others scrambled aboard quickly, with the Cat's sprite fluttering round their heads. She sighed with relief as the dragon took off again. Then the Education Webtown dissolved into a storm of sparkles and in its place she saw the tall red mountains of Dragonville.

'Well done, Leni!'

'Eight!'

Eleni glowed with pride. Cat's sprite, wildly excited now, led the way as the dragon flew on and on between the towering mountains. It all looks pretty much the same, Eleni thought. Where can we be going? Then they flew over a high ridge, and there, below, was an enormous face that filled the valley from side to side. Now she knew where they were going, and wished she didn't. A shiver ran through her as the gigantic mouth opened to let them in, and gulped them down into the darkness.

The dragon shook itself, and Eleni found herself falling. She didn't fall far, and landed with a jolt on cold rock. She was in a gloomy tunnel, lit by a soft glow that came through an archway about twenty metres away. When she picked herself up, she saw Rom and Jack nearby, but the dragon had vanished. Rom groaned. 'Great. *Now* what do we do?'

From above Jack's head came an urgent, angry chittering. 'Get off!' He batted at Cat's sprite, who was dive-bombing him and pulling at his hair. 'We follow this dratted creature, I suppose,' he shrugged. 'At least it seems to know where it's going.'

'And at least it's heading for the light,' Eleni said.

Through the archway there was nothing but a huge old door at the top of a long flight of steps. It stood alone there, looking odd with no walls to support it. Jack went up the steps, followed by Rom and Eleni. He pushed open the heavy, creaking door, and found himself in a huge, circular hallway, with doors leading off it in every direction and a spiral staircase in the centre that led up to galleries with rooms leading off *them*, that stretched up and up as far as the eye could see. Just inside the door, hanging on the wall, he found a rack of heavy-looking guns like laser rifles that glowed with their own eerie red light. A d-box floated in the air beside it. Jack read:

LEVEL 2 ENTRY. Welcome to the Labyrinth, domain of the shifters. Here lies the secret heart of Dragonville. Caution. Gun must be recharged after every five shots.

Next to this was a picture of a red crystal, about half the size of an egg. When he broke open a gun and checked it, Jack found a tube with one red crystal nestling inside.

'Knowing Anna,' Rom said, taking a gun for himself and handing one to Eleni, 'more crystals will be hidden all over the house in the most unlikely places.'

A ghastly shriek ripped through the air, startling Jack into firing off his first shot and wasting it. He spun round, gripping the gun tightly. A white shape, all flowing robes and long streaming hair, came hurtling down from above, reaching for him with bloodstained fingernails as long as knives. Jack ducked and rolled, and the banshee hit the floor. With an ear-splitting screech it sprang up and came at him again, its dark eyes glittering with menace, its deadly fingers reaching for his throat.

As Jack scrambled backward, both Rom and Eleni aimed and fired. Thin, sizzling red beams leaped out – and the banshee kept on coming. Backing away, Jack fired his own gun, but it made no difference. This is wrong, he thought desperately, dodging the clawing fingers by a hair's breadth. It's just a game. My mum's friend *invented* this creature!

It almost had him pinned against the staircase now. Jack leaped aside just too late and one razor-sharp finger caught his arm. He felt the sleeve rip, then a sharp pain stabbed his arm. Jack looked down and saw a thin line of blood. *This couldn't be happening!* No one ever got hurt in the Web – it just wasn't possible. Except that it had happened now.

CHAPTER FOURTEEN
GHOST OF A CHANCE

Jack didn't know whether the injury would affect his Realworld body, but it certainly *hurt*. He realized that this was no longer a game, and they were all in great danger. The temptation to scuttle was overwhelming, but he knew that they would never have another chance to get into the game. If they wanted to find Cat and uncover the mystery of the thief, this was their only chance. 'Let's get out of here,' he yelled at the others. Hoping that the spook wouldn't be able to leave the hallway, he dived through the nearest door, Rom and Eleni close behind him with the banshee snatching at their heels.

Jack slammed the door in the banshee's face. On the other side, the screeching and wailing grew to an ear-splitting pitch, and he could hear the creature's blood-stained talons scrabbling at the barrier. Stained with *his* blood now, Jack thought. He stepped back quickly, worried that the door wouldn't keep the creature out, but after a moment, he realized that he had been right. The banshee couldn't go beyond the First Level hall-way.

'This is Level 2 all right,' Rom said. 'Those shifters sure are meaner this time around.' He scowled disgustedly at his gun. 'This wretched thing is useless,' he said.

'Whoever has been tampering with this game must have disabled the weapons,' Jack added.

'Even so, I feel better with a weapon of some kind,' Eleni

told them. 'Besides, there may be something further on that it *will* hit.'

'You never know,' said Jack. Privately he doubted it, but, although the gun had been useless so far, he certainly didn't want to let go of the only weapon he had. With the others, he began to search the room for more crystals to recharge it, but there weren't that many places to look. This time, they had stepped into a ballroom, with a dusty floor, mirrors all along the walls, and a line of chandeliers, festooned with cobwebs, hanging from the ceiling. Spindly little chairs with gold backs and legs and fat red cushions were lined up around the edges of the dance floor. There were no windows here, so they couldn't escape that way. The only other way out was a door at the far end of the room. Only one of the chandeliers seemed to be working, and that was very dim. Jack ran down the right-hand side of the ballroom, throwing the stupid little chairs aside in his frantic search for more crystals.

'Listen,' Eleni said suddenly. 'Music. Can you hear it?'

It was very faint at first, some kind of waltz played on an old-fashioned synthesizer. Even as Jack stopped to listen, it grew louder, and then, behind the tune, he began to hear a scratching, scuffling noise. In the thick dust of the ballroom floor, footprints began to appear, making swirling tracks in the carpet of dusty grey. Ghostly feet were dancing – only two sets at first, then four, then suddenly there were dozens. Rom, Jack and Eleni crowded close together for moral support. Jack looked up, and his fingers tightened around the gun. He could see clear reflections of the whirling dancers in the mirrors along the wall but when he looked back at the actual room, he saw nothing there but the prints.

The music faltered, and stopped. As one, the feet stopped dancing. Suddenly, the footprints were all pointing in his direction. In the mirror, Jack saw the dancers beginning to move forward until they were closing in on him. He saw their pale, bloodless faces, their wild, dark hair, and their long fangs that gleamed against their blood-red lips. He turned and fled, dashing through the new door before the vampires caught him. This time, the others were in front of him. He slammed the door behind him with a gasp of relief.

The room they had entered seemed to be some kind of study, with a bright fire in the hearth and tall bookshelves that lined the walls. To Jack's right there was a curtained window, and beneath it stood a heavy old desk with a green leather top.

'Good, lots of hiding places here,' Rom said in an unsteady voice. 'Surely there'll be crystals for the gun, and maybe we'll even find some other weapons.'

'The desk seems the most obvious place to look,' Eleni said.

Jack thought it was maybe too obvious, but he said nothing. She looked as though the vampires had given her a bad scare and he didn't want to upset her. 'Come on,' he told her, 'it's worth a try.'

Much to Jack's surprise, it turned out that Eleni was right. In the bottom drawer he found a handful of the power crystals. 'Here!' he yelled at Rom and Eleni.

All three of them were down on their knees, scrabbling in the drawer for crystals when Jack began to get an uneasy feeling that they were not alone. Slowly, he raised his head above the level of the desk and looked around. A thin, pale smoke seemed to be drifting with ease through the solid wall to the right. Once inside the room, it drifted down to make a misty white pool on the floor, and then began to pile itself up again in the form of a rough column. Near the top of the column, two slanting red eyes appeared.

Jack ducked down behind the desk, rolled underneath, and came up firing. Rom leaped up to stand beside him, and Eleni was shooting from behind the desk. The red bolts from their guns just went right through the creature's smoky body. The apparition laughed, a weird, spine-chilling cackle, and began to ooze slowly towards them. Where it had passed, every surface was covered with a film of glittering frost.

'Come on, Eleni, don't get trapped behind there!' Jack grabbed her by the hand and dodged around the apparition, pulling her after him. He made a dive for the window, but there was no escape that way. There was nothing beyond but thick darkness. He couldn't break the glass by firing at it with the gun. Using it to hit the window didn't work either. And the spectre was right behind him!

'It's useless!' Rom, in the far corner, threw away his empty gun. Retreating quickly, Jack looked for a way out. He realized he'd made a serious mistake. There *was* no way out of the room save for the door that led back to the vampires, and if he got through them, he would have to deal with the banshee.

But there must be another way to escape. Jack knew how Anna worked. She would never leave a dead-end like this! Still backing away from the apparition, he looked wildly around the room, hoping for inspiration. There was something familiar about the fireplace, with its high mantelpiece and the two candlesticks, one on either end. Suddenly, he remembered a funny old movie that he had watched with Anna and his parents a while ago. It had a fireplace just like this, and, if he remembered rightly, they tilted one of the candlesticks like a lever and—

The apparition was almost on him. Jack grabbed the candlestick and pulled. A section of the wall beside the fireplace swivelled round to reveal the dark opening of a secret passage. 'Yes!' Jack shouted. 'Come on!' He pushed Rom and Eleni inside and dived through after them, sighing with relief as the secret door grated shut behind him. Only then did he realize that he should have brought the other candlestick. The tunnel was pitch dark.

Well, there was no going back now. Jack began to shuffle down the narrow passage, feeling his way along by touching the walls on either side. For a minute or two everything seemed fine, until he noticed that he could see his hands on either side of him, and the shadowy shapes of Eleni and Rom in front. The walls were beginning to glow with a faint, sickly green light, and he could feel sticky wet slime under his fingers. Something snatched at Jack's outstretched hand. The green slime was growing out from the wall and stretching into a forest of long waving tentacles, all along the passage.

This wasn't how it should work. This couldn't be happening! He couldn't go back, there were too many horrors in the rooms behind him. Before he knew what was happening, Eleni's nerve broke. She fired a volley of shots down the passage, and ran, with Rom a step behind her. Jack took off after them. The tentacles snatched at him, hissing like a thousand snakes. They fastened themselves to his body in a clammy embrace, spattering him with slime that burned his skin. Even as he struggled to free himself, he heard the secret door grate open behind him.

With the strength of panic, Jack tore himself loose and ran on, fighting his way through the clusters of long, clinging arms. The pale gleam of the tentacles gave him enough light to see by, but he didn't dare look back and see what was behind him. He plunged headlong down the twisting passage, shielding his face from the horrid touch of the writhing strands.

He didn't see the wall until it was too late. Jack smashed into the solid barrier just as the others had done and slid to the ground beside them, half stunned and cold with fear. *There was no way out!*

There must be! There *must* be! Jack struggled to his feet and began to poke and prod frantically at the wall. When that didn't work, he fired his gun at it again and again, until he ran out of power. When the noise of the shots had stopped, he realized that he could hear a soft, dry, rustling noise in the passage behind him. Jack recognized it from the ballroom. It was the whisper of many voices, and the shuffle of dozens of feet.

Suddenly, the soft scuffle was drowned out by a hideous shriek. Jack froze, his fingers locked around the useless gun. Not the banshee too! The first thing he saw though, drifting around the bend in the passage, was the wispy form of the red-eyed spook. The eyes glowed brighter as they saw him, and the apparition gave the same, grim, spine-chilling cackle. The ghosts had found him, all of them.

The spectre drifted towards Jack down the length of the corridor, and behind it came the horde of shuffling vampires, visible now, and drooling. As they passed, the snake-like tentacles writhed and hissed, dripping slime in glowing pools on the passage floor. Then the ghastly shriek came again. Jack yelled and pressed himself back into the hard stone of the wall as the banshee plunged down into the passage from the ceiling above. Behind it, the vampires and the cold, misty spectre kept on coming.

CHAPTER FIFTEEN

BATTLE OF DRAGONS

Maxus touched his wrist, and the shifters disappeared. Taking Cat by the hand, he led her back to the pile of crystals and sat down beside her. He began to speak in a gentle voice. 'Let me explain what has happened.'

'She's stealing my *body*?' Cat gasped. 'But that's impossible!'

'You have to understand,' Maxus said gently. 'For Miss Aldanar, nothing is impossible. The Web was her brain-child. She was one of its very first creators. Hers is a brilliant mind that has spanned two centuries,' he went on proudly. 'She spent years developing the equipment you saw in the tower to achieve her greatest triumph yet, the cheating of death itself.'

Cat wanted to hit him. 'It's cheating all right,' she shouted. 'She isn't cheating death, Maxus, she's cheating *me*! She's *had* her life, longer than most people. I've only started mine. Maybe I could have been as brilliant and successful and powerful as she is, but now I'll never know! Miss Aldanar has cheated me of the chance. Don't you understand, Maxus? She hasn't conquered death, she's only making an exchange. Somebody dies in any case! *Somebody always has to die!*'

'BE SILENT, BRAT!' The dragon shrieked.

Maxus looked stunned. 'But she's right,' he cried. 'Madam, is there no other way?'

'If there was, would I be doing this?' the dragon snarled.

'How can you, of all people, think I *want* to act like some kind of ghoul? There's no more time, you imbecile! I CAN'T DIE!' The dragon loomed over Maxus, its jaws gaping wide and its jewelled eyes flashing red with the fire of its rage.

With a terrible cry of fear and sorrow, he hit his scuttle button and vanished.

In the darkness of the tunnel Eleni felt a hard, lumpy shape beneath her. She groped in the darkness, and burst out laughing. 'Guess what?' she shouted. 'I'm sitting on a handle. There's a trapdoor here.'

Spurred by sheer terror, none of them had ever moved quicker. In an instant they had lifted the trapdoor. There was no time to worry about the drop or the darkness, not with the horrors that pursued them. If they had to take their chance with the spooks or the trapdoor there was only one choice. Squeezing through one by one, they took a deep breath, and let themselves fall.

Eleni found herself hurtling down a long, slippery chute, moving faster and faster and unable to stop. Suddenly, she came rocketing out into the light and hurtled into a pile of lumpy, glittering objects that were very hard. She lay still for a moment, recovering, not daring to look up and see what else was in store.

'Holy MIPs!' Rom muttered in an awestruck voice.

Now what? Eleni thought. Steeling herself, she looked up, and up, and up, and up – at an enormous golden dragon.

'Jack! Rom, Eleni!' Cat was running towards them, shrieking. 'Get away! Quick, before it's too late!'

'It is already too late.' The voice sounded like the hollow clang of a dungeon door. Eleni looked at the dragon and saw the great red gem that glittered on a golden chain around the creature's neck. She thought of a tall, dark-haired woman all dressed in silver, and wearing a silver mask. 'I remember you—' she gasped.

The woman glanced at her briefly. 'Well, I don't

remember you,' she said in an offhand voice. She turned her
cold dark gaze on Rom, who seemed unable to take his eyes
from her. '*You*, however, I remember all too well. *Your* day of
reckoning is long overdue.' Her huge mouth opened in an
ear-splitting roar. Twin beams of light, sizzling red, shot out
of her glimmering eyes. With a yell, Rom hurled himself
aside. The lasers hit just where he'd been standing, melting
the stone floor into a pool of glowing slag.

Howling in thwarted fury, the dragon reared up until its
shoulders touched the ceiling. The great head snaked out on
the long neck and another red beam sizzled through the air.
Again, Rom dodged, but he was running out of space.

'Split up!' Cat yelled. 'It's not a game! *She can kill us!*'

'That's enough!' Jack yelled. 'Scuttle!'

'I can't,' Cat shouted. 'They stole my unit!'

Eleni knew they couldn't leave her. Somehow, they must
find a way to defeat this monster and free their friend. She
remembered how the shifters had hurt Jack. She wasn't sure
whether people could really be killed in the Web, but it
would be better not to find out. She didn't know how the
Sorceress had done it, but things were somehow more *real*
here than was usual in the Web. That was it! Like in
Realworld, things could be changed from within the game.

The dragon, snarling, had backed Rom into a corner. Eleni
could see its ruby eyes gleam brighter as it prepared to
fire.

'Rom! Scuttle!' Jack was yelling.

'No!' Rom looked terrified but held his ground.

Suddenly, Eleni knew what to do. She hit her keypad, and
there were *two* golden dragons in the chamber. Red beams
leaped from Eleni's eyes. The Sorceress howled in agony,
beating with one wing at her smoking hide. Leaving Rom,
she whipped round to face her new challenger, knocking
Jack and Cat back into a corner with the tip of her lashing
tail.

Even as the Sorceress turned, Eleni was firing again,

missing the other dragon's head by a hair's breadth and
knocking a chunk of stonework off the far wall.

'Eight, Leni, 'way to go!' Rom shouted.

'Be careful!' Jack yelled.

The Sorceress fired wildly, and Eleni screamed in shock as
the crimson beam snicked the edge of one wing. Mad with
rage, the Sorceress attacked, taking advantage of Leni's
moment of distraction. Drawing her head back, she struck
like a snake and fastened her huge spiked teeth in Eleni's
neck. Eleni screamed and struggled to free herself, but it was
no good. The Sorceress held her fast, and slowly, as the great
jaws tightened, she found herself choking for breath. It was
no good, she would have to scuttle. She had failed.

Out of the corner came a shriek from the Cat. 'It's back!
My unit!'

The dragon loosed its jaws from Eleni's throat. For an
instant, surprise and doubt gleamed in its eyes. Then it
threw back its head and began to laugh. 'And Maxus called
me cruel! Go on, then, my dear. Spin out of here if you wish,
if you dare. Spin back into my aged body, and see how *you*
like life as a withered crone, always growing weaker, always
in pain. *You* try it, Cat, then tell me what I did was wrong!'

Cat looked at her with an oddly pitying expression. 'It *was*
wrong,' she said, in a brave, firm little voice, 'and whatever
you say won't make it right. You have to live with that.'
Then she pressed her keypad, and was gone.

'Scuttle, everyone,' Jack yelled. He and Rom vanished, but
Eleni was a second too late. Before she could move, the
dragon's jaws had clamped round her neck once more.

'You at least, I'll keep,' the Sorceress snarled through her
teeth.

'You won't!' Eleni choked, groping with her claw for her
keypad. Yes, she could just reach it. Lifting her head, she
fired her lasers straight at the ceiling above the other dragon.
Even as it exploded and tons of rock came crashing down,
she hit her scuttle button and caught a glimpse of the

Sorceress doing the same. As the world dissolved around her, the last thing she heard was a shattering cry of utter horror.

'No! NO! MAXUUUUUUS!'

CHAPTER SIXTEEN

AFTERWARDS

As Cat ripped her visor away, the tower room wrapped itself around her like a secure and comfortable quilt. Still numb with shock and terror, she simply sat there for a moment, staring in front of her. Staring— Staring— Staring at the usual view she saw when she spun out, the body of Miss Aldanar, reclining in its Websuit on the couch directly opposite.

Maxus was slumped over the couch, his shoulders shaking. Cat realized that he was crying like a heartbroken child. Slipping out of her Websuit, she went over to him. When she drew near to Miss Aldanar's couch, she realized that the old woman's body was utterly still, no longer breathing. The connections to her life-support machines had been ripped away. Cat touched him gently on the shoulder. 'It was you, wasn't it?' she said softly. 'Thank you, Maxus. You saved my life.'

Maxus lifted a tear-streaked face to look at her. It gave Cat a funny feeling in the pit of her stomach to see a grown-up cry like that, as though nothing would ever be secure in the world again. 'All the stuff she stole,' he whispered brokenly, 'she meant to use it for you, she said.' His voice grew stronger. 'She was working on a way to clone a new body, then you could have yours back, if you could survive that long in the Web. She wanted to put your consciousness into that dragon for the time being. It's a very advanced construct, and she thought you might be spared the fading we had with the other children.'

'*Other children?*,' Cat gasped.

Maxus nodded. 'Don't ask,' he said. 'You were different, you were so much like her. She was fond of you, really she was.'

She picked a funny way to show it, Cat thought, but Maxus was still talking. 'She promised me she would give you your body back, but—' he sighed. 'Seeing her, listening to her today, when she thought she had triumphed, well, suddenly I stopped believing her.'

Gently, he took the old woman's hands and folded them on her breast. 'Truly, she wasn't always bad,' he said softly. 'In her time she was a very great, good woman, but she was always afraid to die. It obsessed her.' He shook his head. 'No matter what she did or how long she lived, that fear would haunt her. In the end I had to help her to be free, just as I always helped her.'

It was several days before everyone could meet again. It had taken that long for the authorities to clear up the mess the Sorceress had left behind her. Eventually, it was arranged for the four friends to get together at Tropicana Bay, along with Anna, released now from the clutches of the police, and Ariadne, the Webcop who had been investigating the Sorceress from the start.

Cat was glad of a chance to talk to the cop. One question had been bothering her a good deal. 'What about Maxus?' she asked anxiously. 'I know he helped Miss Aldanar, but he was the one who stopped her in the end. And after all, he *did* save my life.'

Today, Ariadne was tall with skin like ebony silk, an athletic body, and eyes of liquid gold. Her smile flashed white as she answered. 'Don't worry, Cat, everything has been taken into account. They won't be too hard on him.'

'Will the game ever open again?' Eleni asked Anna. The woman gave a rueful shrug. 'I'm afraid not, Leni, at least not in that form. You seem to have made a pretty good job of destroying it.'

'Anna, I'm sorry!' Eleni cried in dismay.

Anna laughed. 'It's all right, Leni, I'm only teasing. You did the best possible thing, and you were incredibly brave. The authorities won't let me re-open Dragonville anyway. They tell me I was a bit too clever for my own good, inventing a bunch of highly advanced phaces that could sneak through into other sites.'

'You were lucky to get away with it really,' Ariadne told her, 'but with the Sorceress gone, everyone is feeling especially lenient.'

'Now, wait a minute,' Anna protested. 'It wasn't *my* fault if my game was hijacked. *You* couldn't catch her, so I don't see—'

'Peace, peace,' Ariadne held up her hands. 'You're right on all counts. I was only teasing *you*.' She grinned at Anna, and Eleni could see that the two women were well on the way to becoming good friends.

'What happened to all the stuff that was stolen?' Rom asked.

Ariadne shrugged. 'Lost, I'm afraid, in Eleni's explosion. No one is going to start dismantling the game to find the missing data. We're too afraid of activating the shifters again, by accident. The game has been sealed off, in the hope that the stuff can be recovered some day in the future.'

Jack caught Cat's eye, and the two of them left the table and slipped away along the crimson sands. 'How is your father doing?' he asked.

'When the police discovered what had been going on at home, they arranged for him to see doctors and shrinks and stuff.' Cat shrugged, trying to sound as if she didn't care. 'They say he'll get over this hatred of the Web and be perfectly fine, eventually. In the meantime, I have to go with my brothers and sister to stay with some relation I've never even met.' Now, she couldn't keep the quiver out of her voice.

'No you don't,' Jack said quickly. 'Anna and I were talking about it last night, and she suggested that you come to Ireland and stay with her for a while. She asked me to ask you—'

The rest of his words were drowned in Cat's whoop of delight. 'Jack! Is it true? Do you mean it?'

Jack nodded. 'And I'll be just down the road,' he told her. 'We can do all sorts of things, both in the Web and out.'

Cat laughed out loud for sheer joy. 'Oh, this is wonderful! I can't believe it! I must go and thank Anna!'

They got back to the table just in time to hear Rom's voice. 'Anna, do you think she really could have killed us?'

'Who knows?' Anna replied. 'Her abilities were far beyond anything we've seen before. Let's just say it's a good thing we never had to find out.'

Rom looked startled for a moment, then he smiled. 'Well, who cares? I guess that's the end of the Sorceress.'

Ariadne nodded. 'Miss Aldanar is finished at long last, thanks to you lot.'

In another part of the Web, sealed deep within the shattered ruins of an abandoned game, a dragon raised its golden head. '*Am I still alive?*' it thought, and, '*How long will it take me to escape from this tomb?*'

Well, it didn't matter, really, how long it would take. At last, the dragon possessed what it wanted, all the time in the world.

Carefully, the dragon began to examine its prison. Cat would have recognized the stubborn, fierce and proud intelligence trapped behind those glittering ruby eyes.

WEBSPEAK – A GLOSSARY

AI Artificial intelligence. Computer programs that appear to show intelligent behaviour when you interact with them.

avatar or realoe Personas in the Web that are representations of real people.

basement-level Of the lowest level possible. Often used as an insult, as in 'You've got a basement-level grasp of the situation.'

bat The moment of transition into the Web or between sites. You can 'do a bat' or 'go bat'. Its slang use has extended to the everyday world. 'Bat' is used instead of 'come in', 'take a bat' is a dismissal. (From *Blue And Tone*.)

bite To play a trick, or to get something over on someone.

bootstrap Verb, to improve your situation by your own efforts.

bot Programs with AI.

chasing the fade Analysing what has happened in the Web after you have left it.

cocoon A secret refuge. Also your bed or own room.

cog	Incredibly boring or dull. Initially specific to the UK and America this slang is now in use worldwide. (From *Common Or Garden* spider.)
curl up	'Go away, I don't like you!' (From *curl up and die*.)
cyberat	A Web construct, a descendant of computer viruses, that infests the Web programs.
cybercafe	A place where you can get drinks and snacks as well as renting time in the Web.
cyberspace	The visual representation of the communication system which links computers.
d-box	A data-box; an area of information which appears when people are in Virtual Reality (VR).
download	To enter the Web without leaving a Realworld copy.
down the plug	A disaster, as in 'We were down the plug'.
egg	A younger sibling or annoying hanger-on. Even in the first sense this is always meant nastily.
eight	Good (a spider has eight legs).
flame	An insult or nasty remark.
fly	A choice morsel of information, a clue, a hint.
funnel	An unexpected problem or obstacle.
gag	Someone, or something, you don't like very much, whom you consider to be stupid. (From *Glove And Glasses*.)

glove and glasses   Cheap but outdated system for experiencing Virtual Reality. The glasses allow you to see VR, the gloves allow you to pick things up.

Id   Interactive display nodule.

mage   A magician.

mip   Measure of computer power.

nick or alias   A nickname. For example, 'Metaphor' is the nickname of Sarah.

one-mip   Of limited worth or intelligence, as in 'a one-mip mind'.

phace   A person you meet in the Web who is not real; someone created by the software of a particular site or game.

phreak   Someone who is fanatical about virtual reality experiences in the Web.

protocol   The language one computer uses to talk to another.

raid   Any unscheduled intrusion into the Web; anything that forces someone to leave; a program crash.

realoe   See *avatar*.

Realworld   What it says; the world outside the Web. Sometimes used in a derogatory way.

scuttle   Leave the Web and return to the Realworld.

silky   Smarmy, over-enthusiastic, un-trustworthy.

six   Bad (an insect has six legs).

slows, the   The feeling that time has slowed down after experiencing the faster time of the Web.

spider	A Web construct. Appearing in varying sizes and guises, these are used to pass on warnings or information in the Web. The word is also commonly applied to teachers or parents.
spidered-off	Warned away by a spider.
spin in	To enter the Web or a Website.
spin out	To leave the Web or a Website.
SFX	Special effects.
strand	A gap between rows of site skyscrapers in Webtown. Used to describe any street or road or journey.
suck	To eat or drink.
supertime	Parts of the Web that run even faster than normal.
TFO	Tennessee Fried Ostrich.
venomous	Adjective; excellent; could be used in reference to piece of equipment (usually a Websuit) or piece of programming.
vets	Veterans of any game or site. Ultra-vets are the *crème de la crème* of these.
VR	Virtual Reality. The illusion of a three-dimensional reality created by computer software.
warlock	A sorcerer; magician.
Web	The worldwide network of communication links, entertainment, educational and administrative sites that exists in cyberspace and is represented in Virtual Reality.
Web heads	People who are fanatical about surfing the Web. (See also phreaks.)

Web round   Verb; to contact other Web users via
                       the Web.

Websuit   The all-over body suit lined with
                       receptors which when worn by Web
                       users allows them to experience the
                       full physical illusion of virtual
                       reality.

Webware   Computer software used to create
                       and/or maintain the Web.

widow   Adjective; excellent; the term comes
                       from the Black Widow, a particu-
                       larly poisonous spider.

wipeout   To be comprehensively beaten in a
                       Web game or to come out worse in
                       any Web situation.

OTHER TITLES IN
THE WEB SERIES

GULLIVERZONE by Steve Baxter

February 7, 2027, World Peace Day. It's a day of celebration everywhere. Even access to the Web is free today. It's the chance Sarah's been waiting for, a chance to sample the most wicked sites, to visit mind-blowing virtual worlds. She chooses GulliverZone and the chance to be a giant amongst the tiny people of Lilliput.

But the peace that is being celebrated in the real world does not extend into cyberspace. There is a battle for survival being fought in Lilliput and what Sarah discovers there in one day will be enough to change her life for ever – providing she can get out to live it . . .

GULLIVERZONE, the fear is anything but virtual.

GULLIVERZONE, ready for access.

FEEL UP TO ANOTHER?

DREAMCASTLE by Stephen Bowkett

Dreamcastle is the premier fantasy role-playing site on the Web, and Surfer is one of the premier players. He's one of the few to fight his way past the 500th level, one of the few to take on the Stormdragon and win. But it isn't enough, Surfer has his eyes on the ultimate prize. He wants to be the best, to discover the dark secret at the core of Dreamcastle. And he's found the girl to take him there. She's called Xenia and she's special, frighteningly special.

He's so obsessed that he's blind to Rom's advice, to Kilroy's friendship and to the real danger that lies at the core of the Dreamcastle. A danger that could swallow him whole . . . for real.

DREAMCASTLE, it's no fantasy.

DREAMCASTLE, ready for access.

THINK YOU'RE UP TO IT?

UNTOUCHABLE by Eric Brown

Life might be easier for most people in 2027 but for Ana Devi, whose only home is the streets of New Delhi, it's a battle for survival. She's certainly never dreamed of visiting the bright virtual worlds of the Web. And when her brother is kidnapped the Web is certainly the last thing she is thinking about. But the Web holds the secret to what has happened to her brother and to dozens of other New Delhi street children.

How can Ana possibly find enough money to access the Web when she can barely beg enough to eat each day? Who will help her when her caste means that no one will even touch her? Somehow she must find a way or she will never see her brother again.

Dare you touch the truth of UNTOUCHABLE?

UNTOUCHABLE, ready for access.

TAKE ANOTHER WALK ON THE WILD SIDE

SPIDERBITE by Graham Joyce

In 2027, a lot of schooltime is Webtime. Imagine entering Virtual Reality and creeping through the Labyrinth with the roars of the Minotaur echoing in your ears? Nowhere near as dull as the classroom. The sites are open to all, nothing is out of bounds. So why has Conrad been warned off the Labyrinth site? There shouldn't be any secrets in Edutainment.

Who is behind the savage spiders that swarm around Conrad whenever he tries to enter the site? And why do none of his friends see them? There is a dark lesson being taught at the centre of the Labyrinth . . .

SPIDERBITE, school was never meant to be this scary . . .

SPIDERBITE, ready for access.

ARE YOU READY TO GO AGAIN?

LIGHTSTORM by Peter F. Hamilton

Ghostly lights out on the marsh have been the subject of tales and rumours for as long as anyone can remember but the reality is far more frightening than any ghost story. Something is going wrong at the nearby energy company and they are trying to keep it a secret. Somebody needs to be told. But Aynsley needs help to do it. The Web keeps him in touch with a network of friends across the world and it might just offer him a way in past the company security to find out exactly what's going on.

But the Web works both ways. If Aynsley can get to

the company then the company can get to him. And the company has a way of dealing with intruders.

LIGHTSTORM, sometimes it's best to be in the dark.

LIGHTSTORM, ready for access.